S.W.A.T.

S.W.A.T.

A NOVELIZATION BY DIANE CAREY
BASED ON THE SCREENPLAY BY
RON MITA & JIM MCCLAIN AND DAVID AYER
STORY BY GEORGE HUANG

POCKET STAR BOOKS
New York   London   Toronto   Sydney   Singapore

An *Original* Publication of POCKET BOOKS

A Pocket Star Book published by
POCKET BOOKS, a division of Simon & Schuster, Inc.
1230 Avenue of the Americas, New York, NY 10020

Copyright © 2003 Columbia Pictures Industries, Inc.
All rights reserved.

Cover art copyright © 2003 Columbia Pictures Industries, Inc.
All rights reserved.

ISBN: 0-7434-6771-X

First Pocket Books printing July 2003

10   9   8   7   6   5   4   3   2   1

POCKET STAR BOOKS and colophon are registered trademarks of Simon & Schuster, Inc.

Manufactured in the United States of America

For information regarding special discounts for bulk purchases, please contact Simon & Schuster Special Sales at 1-800-456-6798 or business@simonandschuster.com.

This novelization is dedicated, with respect,
to the American law enforcement community,
of which my dad was a proud member.

S.W.A.T.

1

"OFFICER DOWN! MY PARTNER'S HIT! SHOTZZZZZZTTTZZ zzzzomatic gunfire! Suspects have AK-47s and body armor! Nothing we're shooting can stop them! Send S.W.A.T.! Senzzzzzzzzzzzttt—"

THE LOS ANGELES BASIN

Noise, noise, noise. Most days, the city could almost be described as quiet. Brown smog loitered against the white and pink downtown buildings, crawling up toward the HOLLYWOOD sign with its crooked letters against the scruffy hillside, a now-timeless emblem of glitz, struggle, hope, dismay, fame, and ruin. Quiet hope, quiet ruin.

Not today.

Men in sniper gear peppered the streetscape, tucked into the city's cracks. Flak vests, black caps, weapons, shields. Bright daylight and neon signs sprinkled glitter across the pavement and rows of stores and businesses. The empty sidewalk glittered too, but with splinters of valueless shattered glass.

Shots fired. Shots fired. Shots fired.

Terrible words to any police officer's ear.

Police cars lay in a pretense of repose all over the street, both sides. Hazard lights flashed and there was a cop behind every door. They'd managed to yellow-tape two ends of the boulevard, then fell into that eerie silence that seizes up the middle part of any hostage situation. It was the waiting that's not the same as real waiting.

The drama unfolding here had been seen before, but no one could predict the ending and few tried. A news helicopter banked over the city so frantically that its rotors made a painful whine. Police transmissions were laced with gunfire and panic. The chopper picked up the trouble on its scanner, and now the whole city knew something godawful was happening.

No, not one chopper . . . there were a half dozen now, swirling wildly in 3-D. News choppers, traffic choppers—the skies were full of dragonflies jockeying for position over a war zone. Just a bank, really, most days, but today the hub of a storm. Gunfire blew out the shimmer of Southern California's air just as the first news chopper cleared the hills and raced over the big white *W* into the stretching valley below. The chopper swerving like a bug toward the bank parking lot, where its occupants got a shock—the barrel of a machine gun pointed right at them and the flares of fire burping from it.

2

Whether they could hear the sharp *brrrrrddddt* of the AK-47 over the scream of their own noise, none of the choppers' occupants would ever remember. All they saw was the gunfire and only then realized that this wasn't exactly television, where things could be edited out. These were real bullets and they might themselves become the vultures' favorite footage. But that's why they were here, wasn't it? To get those incredible shots?

Shots—rapid, ripping machine-gun fire, cracking the morning air, flung from the weapon of a criminal in bulky black clothing as he ducked behind cars in the bank parking lot. He had successfully caused the helicopters to fly into a frenzy, first avoiding bullets, then avoiding one another.

Two robbers now. They moved through the parking lot, the second being covered by the machine gun of the first. This was a planned event, pretty clearly, a revelation suddenly bright to the cops who were seizing into a hasty perimeter of black-and-whites around the center of action. Sirens cleaved the air as more black-and-whites screamed into place, skidding gracelessly into a weird puzzle. The two robbers kept coming.

Bullets *thunked* into the heavy police cars. The cops, body armor or not, ducked for cover and stayed ducked. Whoever these guys were, they weren't afraid of dying, or of killing.

Patrolman Rudy Tinewood saw all this from the wildest vantage point—his patrol Harley. He skidded into the scene knowing—who could miss it?—

that something was up, but he didn't know what, exactly, and took the motions of two fellow cops to get the hell off his bike and down on the ground as damned fair advice. He hit the pavement, using his motor as cover, and looked between the Harley's tires at the movements of the two bads.

"Get down!" Officer Skip Michaels called to him from the crook of his patrol car's door, where he and his partner huddled together. "We got two suspects inside with hostages! Two just left the bank in head-to-toe armor!"

"S.W.A.T. on the way?" Tinewood barked back, careful not to yell.

"Damned straight!"

That's when Tinewood felt the hard *pok* of force against his pelvis. He was rolling. Rolling . . . the pavement changed color under him, white, then red. His brain registered excitement at all that sudden brightness and splashy change, like a scene from Devan's favorite video game, the one he always played with that goofy best friend of his with the rattail, the champ of the fourth grade. Special effects. Computer blood.

Wasn't it?

They might as well have been riding in the back of a pickup truck, like teenagers enjoying a day playing hooky. This job was just too much fun sometimes. "Fun" included helicopter rides.

Jim Street loved helicopter rides.

He leaned back in the cramped area behind the

4

pilot, forcing his shoulder muscles to relax, and re-arranged his elbow from where it had been gouging his partner's ribs.

Beside him, Brian Gamble was less jovial, somewhere between grim and bored.

Street raised his voice over the chopper's roar. "The lieutenant asked me to give some speech at this high school in Whittier. Can you sub for me?"

"No chance," Gamble bluntly said. "*You* do it."

"If I get in front of more than five people, I totally freeze up, start sweating like a pig!"

"It's a bunch of sixteen-year-old girls. Don't be such a pussy."

"Who's the pussy I have to cuff to the dentist's chair just to get a cavity filled?"

"Fear of dentists' drills is a perfectly acceptable phobia. Fear of high school assemblies isn't."

"Fine," Street said. "Next time, you give the speech and I'll ge the root canal."

"Fine."

The pilot turned and yelled. "Thirty seconds out, boys!"

Street's smile dissolved. He and Gamble pulled on black helmets and each swatted the other on the back of the head for luck and vow—*I'll watch your back.*

"Time to party," Gamble spoke to the wind.

Two blocks down, close enough to see what was going on but far enough to move around, Martin Comstock leaned on the counter of his gun store's

5

front aisle and watched the events unfold on a wall-mounted TV set, every now and then glancing down the street and into the sky to catch a bit of the real thing. No way was he going out there, like the jerks streaking past his store for a firsthand look. Morons. Who runs *toward* a gunfight?

At the front door there was a clatter. He recognized it after ten years and two months in the business. Heavy boots, the creak in the door that only happened when it was wrenched open by a strong arm, the gush of body odor. Men. In a fleeting thought he chided himself for not locking the door. Gunfights could shift location. A gun store could become a target.

Or not. What the hell. Gotta take a chance in life now and then. He forced himself away from his TV set and turned to meet the customers.

What faced him weren't sportsmen or home-defense buffs, but two uniformed L.A.P.D. cops, both breathless and flush-faced.

"You got anything that'll penetrate body armor?" the smaller of the cops demanded. He had a high voice but forceful eyes.

"I'm not allowed by law to sell those kinds of weapons," Comstock told him, repeating a well-rehearsed sentence.

The second cop, the bigger one, huffed and put his hands on his hips. The first cop got squeakier. "What do you got in the back?"

They were serious. They wanted in on that action outside. This wasn't a bust. Comstock glanced at the carnage on the TV screen. Freewheeling crooks with body armor and high-powered automatic weapons. Had one of those weapons arrived at this day's activity in a roundabout route from Comstock's own back room? He tried to be careful who his customers were, but there was nothing he could do about his customers' bad judgment when the guns left their hands. There were guns everywhere, all over the world. There always had been. He remembered his days in grade school back in Idaho. All the boys had rifles in their lockers. There was a hunt club after school every Tuesday and Thursday. Even all these years later he remembered the lessons in firearms safety that took place right in the hallway outside the principal's office. Back then every kid had a gun and every house had one or two. It wasn't the guns that had changed in America. It was something else.

Oh, what the double hell.

He ducked into his back room and came out with a cache of the kinds of weapons he would choose himself if he were one of the cops. Automatic weapons, machine guns, sweet to the hand, firm recoil, true aim, completely illegal to sell. Perfect.

What else were cops supposed to use to return fire when these things were shooting at them? Rubber bands?

"How do you plan on paying for these?" Comstock asked. Might as well lay everything on the line, right?

The squeaky cop barked, "The city'll reimburse

you," and held his hand out for the box of ammunition.

Comstock plunked the box into the man's rosy hand. "For illegal weapons from the back of my shop?"

Just then there was a roar outside, real low, real close. They looked at the ten-foot-tall tempered windows in time to see an L.A.P.D. helicopter swoop low over the Jiffy Lube across the street, heading for the action even as three other choppers raced away.

The two cops glanced at each other. The big one took out his wallet.

"You take Mastercard?"

The L.A.P.D. helicopter was black and glossy, proud of itself. It came with built-in attitude. If the chopper found itself called into action, there was probably a good reason to look racy. The pilots liked the tight feeling of this particular unit. She was a spry young whipper and she liked her job. All the pilots wanted her.

Today she was loaded for bear, hungry for action, and up to the gills with firepower, but not with mounted weaponry. She wasn't a fighter jet. She was a warhorse with soldiers aboard. She peeled in, made one graceful spin, leveled off, and hovered with style—a helicopter's best trick—over the flat-roofed two-story bank. The two hatches opened in her sides, and out sprang four men, fast-roping down like spiders fleeing the wind. Their boots hit the tar-paper roof at almost the same instant. They disengaged from the drop lines and were running within the first two seconds. The helicopter wheeled overhead and roared away, leaving the four Special Weapons and Tactics officers on their own. No backup was in any S.W.A.T. plan. They were one another's backup, and everybody else's.

Jim Street kept repeating that to himself as he and partner Brian Gamble split off from the other two team officers, who had taken up cover positions. Street and Gamble went straight to the roof hatch that would get them down to where the gunfire was going on. They could hear it, short and shitty and coming in burps below. As Gamble jammed his breaching gun into the hatch's locking mechanism and set the charge, Street let his opinion, and some of the emotion behind it, out.

"I hate AKs," he said, squinting against the bright sunlight. He felt his teeth grind a little. Keep control . . .

"They're shooting cops," Gamble said. "We should be down there."

"Bank full of hostages says otherwise."

Gamble didn't answer, but pushed Street back a couple of steps and ticked off seconds under his breath.

The hatch exploded with a severe *POP*. "Me first," Street claimed.

"You were first last time," Gamble protested.

"Don't make me smack you."

"Get in the hole." Gamble actually smiled as he waved to the other two S.W.A.T. officers, motioning them to follow as Street disappeared into the bank's ductwork.

Two, three, four—they followed into the darkness, with the sounds of *tack tack tack tack tack* gunfire chasing them all the way.

"Got a visual."

Lieutenant Gregory Velasquez huddled in a quickie command post set up behind a police truck kitty-corner from a gun shop in a strip mall. From here, just with his naked eyes, he could see the little black heads of at least two bad guys shuttling in and out of parked cars next to the bank. The red-alert lights of a half dozen black-and-whites—at least that's how many he could see from here—flashed frantically and added an urgent drama to the sound of those AKs. He got the crawlies as he saw the bodies of several downed cops, not moving, at least six more taking cover, and two uniforms just now running out of the gun shop with high-powered weapons in their hands. Where did those two jokers think they were going?

He ignored them and concentrated on his own officers and the rough plan he had in his head.

"Is everyone in position?" he asked the technical specialist at his side as they watched the skittish closed-circuit monitor with the visual of the crime scene.

"Almost," the sergeant responded.

"We cut off their phones?"

"Yes, sir."

"Send in the secure phone."

"Understood."

Velasquez paused as his order was followed. He wanted to keep talking—it helped—but he knew he had to clam up every few seconds just to keep a clear head and understand what was happening. He glanced at the strip mall's roof, just over the gun shop. He could just see the top of Paul Alvarez's head, and the head and shoulders of Alvy's spotter, a ruddy burly mick named Taylor. Taylor had binoculars up to his eyes and was scanning the action, spotting for Alvarez, who was staring with that Zen-thing snipers get.

Velasquez tried to think like them. Targets on foot . . . behind a car . . . some reflection on the windshields . . .

"Don't let 'em get in a car, boys," Velasquez murmured.

"Sir?" the tech sergeant looked up at him, squinting into the sun behind Velasquez.

"Nothing, not you. Just communicating telepathically with the sniper. We've got four bad guys, we think, with two of them moving around in that parking lot. If Alvy can take one down, it cuts the chances of escape and reduces our targets by one quarter. Problem is, the parking lot's crowded with cops. If one of those cops jumps at the wrong moment, Alvy could cap him without—hey, hey, they're getting into a car! Sierra One, Sierra One, do not let them get mobile! You copy?"

In his mind he calculated what was happening on the roof. He used to be a sniper's spotter himself and hadn't lost the tricks. Wind at Alvarez's back, three miles an hour . . . distance . . . angle . . . there was a car moving in the bank parking lot!

"Fire," he whispered. "Fire, fire, *fire*—"

"Driver's been neutralized."

Jim Street heard the encouraging report on the faint radio connection in his ear. There wasn't much chatter going on, luckily. When cops chattered over the airways, he felt compromised.

Maybe this was good news, or maybe it wasn't. One of the robbers was down—good—but that could make the others desperate and more unpredictable. Either way, it set him on edge. The situation had just changed, and he was in here with no way to measure the dynamics of the change.

He had no idea how this would end. He'd given up trying to map out the end of this musical he'd been rehearsing for ever since he was a kid making sticks into guns in his mind, or using his hands if he didn't have sticks. Anything could be a gun. The trick—the test of character for any kid—came in choosing whether your stick was the criminal's gun or the cop's gun. The world really was made up of good guys and bad guys, a lesson Street had learned early.

Now the boulevard out there bristled with guns

good and bad, and everybody was waiting for the next change. Every crack was a sniper's nest with a gleaming black barrel poking from it, leading down the black tunnel to ballistics and aching to blow. Street counted off the seconds in a time schedule of his own choosing, judging the voice of the barricaded criminals and the mellow counterpoint of the police negotiator.

He flexed his shoulders and adjusted his earpiece and throat mike. He felt hot. No way around that. This was L.A., the land of sun and more sun. Try dressing in layers of Kevlar, skid gear, combat boots, radio equipment, and a helmet and be Sam Suave at the same time. Funny how your body could adjust, though. He was lucky to have the frame of a skateboarder instead of a wrestler, like Gamble did. He glanced at his partner and noticed that Brian was sweating at the temples.

He pressed his shoulder to the wall and reminded himself of his privilege to be here, with Brian and these other cops on the force, each a world-class athlete at the top of his game.

When they got to the bank's equipment room, Brian Gamble stopped to assemble their cutting torch, and Street motioned to the other two team officers to cover the hallway, then hit his radio's mike. "We're at the equipment room. All set for diversion fire."

"All right," Greg Velasquez responded. "Stand by for diversion fire. Five, four—"

Gamble handed the cutting torch to Street. He

was closer to the part of the floor they had targeted to be cut away. Below them was the room with the hostages.

"—three, two—"

Street and Gamble connected looks for a moment, then listened to the burst of gunfire outside. Street snapped the igniter. Muffled by the street battle outside, he cut into the sheet metal between them and the real action. He cut fast, as fast as science let him.

Below him were a handful of robbers, four in all, if surveillance was right, and an unknown number of hostages. A bank robbery gone wrong. Now one robber was killed and the stakes were ratcheted up. The bad guys knew the cops would do whatever they had to do, and that made the bads angry on top of desperate. They hadn't come here to die, but to steal, and yet dying had to be on the list for anyone who came to a crime scene with body armor on. Street had no apologies to make. Not yet, anyway.

Pok pok pok!

"Flashbang grenades," he murmured to Gamble. "Lieutenant's keeping them distracted."

"Hurry up."

"Yeah, yeah, hurrying—"

"We got a view, boys," Velasquez offered over the noise of grenades and gunfire.

Street didn't stop cutting. "Let's hear what you got."

"I got distraction devices going off all around the

14

guy in the parking lot. . . . He's running. . . . Four S.W.A.T.'s rushing him with M-4 carbines . . . Oh, shit, he's down! That's two! The perps inside are gonna be pissed, betcha."

"Roger that," Street grumbled.

"Keep cutting, man," Gamble suggested, twitching.

Outside they heard the muffled *poom poom poom* of grenades exploding, and the sounds came from different directions. Together Street and Gamble cut the sheet metal studs with aviation snippers, then Gamble peeled back the plaster in one fast crunch. Street winced, hoping the crunch was hidden inside a *poom*, then flinched again when Lieutenant Velasquez's voice broke in their microphones again, seeming as if it came over a loudspeaker.

Street could imagine the kind of conversation the negotiator was trying to get rolling. Chatter, just chatter. Criminals who had these kinds of weapons wouldn't let the fear show in their voices, if they had sense to have fear. They were impossible to negotiate with, he knew.

Still, no hostage situation was routine. You could see the same scenario two hundred times, and the two hundred first would blast away complacency. No point letting things come to that.

Even if Street and the other cops had been through this, and even if the criminals had, he could be sure it was the first time for the hostages.

"Okay, we got three of our guys moving in with bulletproof shields. . . . Almost to the front door . . .

They're coming in with a remote phone for these jokers. Almost there . . . Shit, the bad guys inside just saw the getaway driver's body. They're not gonna be happy."

"Yeah, but I am," Street muttered. Carefully he fed a snake camera into the room below.

Gamble arranged a tiny monitor screen that showed them what was happening in the room down there. The two watched as Street manipulated the camera's eye.

There were the hostages, laid out on the floor, some of them sobbing. *Stay cool, folks, help's a-coming.*

"How the hell are we gonna get out of here!" one of the two remaining bank robbers wailed. He had a rasping voice, like sandpaper, like maybe there was something wrong with his throat, maybe a childhood disease or somebody hit him in the neck and it healed wrong.

Everything fell eerily silent. The grenades stopped popping, the gunfire ceased, the noise outside went away.

Then, a voice.

"We're just bringing in a phone! No shots!"

"Boys, when they get that phone inside, I'm ordering our wounded to be pulled out of the lines of fire. Keep an eye on the perps and tell me what's happening inside."

"Will do," Street acknowledged. "They're at the door." He whispered, careful now to keep his voice down. The slightest shuffle, now that the plaster and steel had been pulled back, could be fatal—for somebody else. There were S.W.A.T. officers at the front door of the bank. If the robbers found out he and Gamble were here, they might feel cornered.

"Put it inside the door and bug your asses away from here!"

This second robber's voice was clear and deep, almost like a radio announcer, but with some kind of accent. Jamaican, Mexican—Street couldn't identify it. Just a little bit—maybe some people wouldn't even hear it at all.

His stomach contracted. If the kidnappers heard so much as a scuff, those hostages were all done and this entire operation could turn into a free-for-all that would fill up the morgue. He hoped there were no squirrels on the roof. He willed himself not to breathe—well, to breathe slowly. If he held his breath, he'd start to gasp.

He tried to iron out the psychology in his mind. He knew there were at least three hostage takers in there, and they would kill cops on sight. He tried to stage the scene in his mind, to have some idea of where they might be standing, how they would have to twist to aim at him or anyone else, where the windows were and other possible exits.

On the monitor, tilted really crooked, Street and Gamble watched a skittish blue-and-white view of the front door as two S.W.A.T. men behind a shield awkwardly pulled the bank's glass door open and pushed in a portable short-range direct-line phone. Then the men simply shut the door and backed away as instructed. Good. No cowboys. Of course, the others knew Street and Gamble were in place. Who needed cowboys when the cavalry was already here?

The other robber, not Rasp, snatched up the phone. The leader, obviously.

"I'm controlling this situation! You hear me?"

"We can get to the lobby," Street murmured, under cover of the perp's own loud voice.

"Ten-David, Street, hold your position. CNT has them on the phone. Stand by."

Just beyond the hole in the wall, innocent hostages whimpered and gasped, sobbed and feared. Street could feel their terror. How many of them were already dead? How many wounded? Were they frail or young or sick? They needed help. He and Gamble were right here. Why wait?

"Ten-David wants us to hold."

Gamble's strong features crumpled. "We hold, they die."

With that, and no other announcement, Brian Gamble simply slipped through the hole into the critical area.

"Guess we're not holding," Street blurted. He murmured a few more selective curses about Gamble's gambling, then skittered through the hole too.

2

"CONFIRM THAT YOU'RE HOLDING, STREET."

In his mind Street could imagine the negotiator trying to talk to the robbers, promising them anything. Helicopters, pizza, cars, leniency. Suddenly he froze. He could hear them!

"—buying us some time! Now go kill that talky bitch and throw her ass in the street so they know we're serious!"

"Come here!"

"No—please!"

Three voices. Rasp, Deep, and a woman.

He slipped to the floor and skittered behind the bank counter and drew close to Gamble, who also was hiding there. They were only a few feet away from the robbers now. Even a whisper would be heard.

"Gamble! Street! Where the hell are you! Why aren't you responding!"

Street clamped his lips and gritted his teeth. The urge to whisper a response was enough to choke a camel. Gamble looked at him. Street mouthed *No shots!* then used his hands to signal his intentions. He would move into position for a better angle. Did Gamble get the idea? They'd been together long enough, he hoped, for his fingers to do the talking.

On stealth mode he shimmied below counter level to the other side of the room, but not exactly opposite Gamble, to make sure they didn't end up in each other's crossfire. The angle had to be just right.

He kept telling himself that out of every S.W.A.T. maneuver involving a real crisis, very few had bloody endings. All cops were egotistical turkeys in a lot of ways, which was why they carried guns, but every one of them took it as a win when he could bury a situation without burying any bodies. The MP-5 submachine gun in Street's hands seemed suddenly warm and alive as he stared into what might be a lose/lose situation. Maybe all they could control was just how much they would lose.

He saw Gamble lining up a shot. The robbers both had body armor and helmets on. They'd come into this bank expecting trouble with cops, obviously. They hadn't expected a clean getaway, or they wouldn't be dressed this way. The trick now was to make sure that the shots he and Gamble fired were effective the first time, not give the robbers a warning and a chance to return fire.

Trouble was, the only spot unexposed was a small slit between the Rasp's helmet and the collar of his bulletproof vest. Just a wedge of skin . . . and he was a moving target. He had a lady up against the front window and was using her as a human shield.

Street started to sweat under his own armor. This was the time when the situation could turn against them. Innocent blood made a grisly skating rink. From Gamble's angle, the lady teller's arm, pulled up around her head by the bad guy, blocked the shot. Every time Rasp took a step, the woman was yanked more in the way of Gamble's aim. Luck wasn't going right.

Street craned his neck—a risk, since it made him another inch taller behind the counter. He didn't know where there might be mirrors in the room, or bits of chrome that might reflect his movements. Even being hidden wasn't a guarantee that you couldn't be seen. "Behind" was relative, especially in a store or bank. People who worked in such places got to know angles very well and often would set up little aids around a room, like silver picture frames or reflective glass vases. Those things could work against anyone trying to do what Street and Gamble were trying.

Peering over the Plexiglas counter, he calculated his angle. He had a clear shot of Rasp, while Gamble couldn't possibly. He tried to signal Gamble, but his partner was all wrapped up in the impossible shot. *Take the other guy! The other guy!*

Now racing against Gamble, Street shivered at the concept of working against his partner. This wasn't the idea, it wasn't the idea at all—

Pok!

Gamble's gun!

The bullet beat Street's shot by a third of a second, long enough for him to pull back and not fire. Gamble's shot slapped through the woman's shoulder and into Rasp's neck. The bad guy dropped like wet cement. The woman staggered and screamed in agony.

The head perp—Deep Voice—was supposed to have been neutralized by Gamble's clear shot, but that shot was wasted on a bad line of sight and now it was too late to correct. Deep swung around, with nobody aiming at him, and swept the lobby with his AK, spraying like a garden hose.

Bullets rattled into the Plexiglas and Street dived for the floor, unable to complete his fleeting chance to shoot the guy. He squirmed up, letting his gun lead the way and regrouped to return fire. Then Deep's hand cramped and the AK stopped shooting for an instant. A chance!

Street jumped up onto the top of the Plexiglas counter and opened fire. He ditched the training that tried to get him to shoot at the body or head and went right for the guy's face. He didn't have any armor on his goddamned face!

The man with the deep voice was blown straight backward, and when he landed he had no eyes or nose. Those features had been punched back into his skull.

Street didn't wait for applause. He skidded the rest of the way over the counter and rushed to the teller, who was slumped against the wall, her arm covered with blood. "Street, Ten-David," he barked into his mike, "the lobby is clear. Two suspects are neutralized. I need an RA unit for a gunshot wound to a hostage." He pulled a first-aid dressing from his vest and pressed it to the stunned woman's wound. "You'll be fine, ma'am. Ambulance is on the way."

When he shifted to look at the other hostages, to be sure they all had their heads up and were moving, instead he found himself looking at Gamble, who was just kneeling beside him. Street gave him an angry look, finally venting the exasperation he'd been holding back.

Gamble saw the look. "Hey, we got 'em, right? She'll be fine."

He was way too happy.

Street started to respond, but was cut off by the rush of S.W.A.T. officers and patrolmen flooding the bank lobby. They were here for cleanup duty.

"Four down, none to go," Gamble crowed.

Bravado yielded to anxiety pretty quickly. Especially when they had to endure a shuttered version of congrats from the other men and women on the force. He could storm a room full of thugs with handguns and blades and butcher knives and spit. No problem. But this sitting out in a hallway, waiting to get chewed out, with your neck strangling in a regulation tie and dress blues with pleats—tough service.

Everybody could tell within minutes what had happened that shouldn't have. There were ten eyewitnesses, the bank in-house cameras, plus the angles of the shots and a dozen other obvious clues. Street and Gamble never even got the chance to write their reports before everybody including the pissy news media had dissected the event and broadcast it worldwide. Within hours there were outcries of the S.W.A.T. hotshots' taking matters into their own hands and going against orders, talk shows were arguing the moral points, the Libertarians were griping about police states, the Republicans were blindly backing the cops, and the Democrats were trying to find a racial angle.

Fact was, Jim Street knew, the event had been a successful screwup. He and Gamble had failed to act in tandem, or wait for a central coordinator to tie up the corners. He was replaying the day in his head—again—when S.W.A.T. officer T. J. McCabe joined him and Gamble as the two of them waited outside Captain Fuller's office for their latest dressing-down.

Yeah, they were used to this. He and Brian Gamble had a reputation for hot-rodding their way through the hard spots, skirting orders, not waiting around for coordinated efforts, taking the shots while they had 'em, and so on. Usually it worked out—that's what Special Weapons and Tactics was all about. Not being predictable. Sometimes people had to die, never mind that they trained inexhaustibly to kill when they needed to. The only bigger part of the training than how to kill was the part about how and when *not* to kill. This time they'd pushed too hard.

Or had they? Wounded cops in the parking lot, AK-47s rattling in the air, almost a dozen hostages inside—who could really judge what was too much and what was not enough? Like after the World Trade Center and Columbine, media loudmouths squawked about how someone "should've known" what was coming. Since when? How could anybody "know"? Big talk from the no-risk crowd, pounding on the closed barn door.

Backseat drivers, hindsight operators—none of them was in that bank with Street and Gamble. Nobody could say, "Cut! Hold positions. Camera off. Let's freeze this event and analyze it, then redraw the blocking so it has the outcome we want."

He shook his head, realizing he was kicking himself before Captain Fuller got the chance to kick him. Gamble was right. The bad guys were destroyed and the hostages weren't. End results mattered.

T. J. McCabe shook him out of his thoughts. "The bosses gonna tear you a new one?"

Street glanced at Gamble, then said, "Same place they tore us one the last time. And the time before that."

"When it's over," McCabe said, "let me buy you guys a beer."

"Yeah, whatever," Gamble muttered inhospitably.

T.J. frowned at his ineffective attempt to show support. "Good luck. You were heroes out there."

It worked on Street. Not on Gamble. When they were alone again, Gamble looked at him and said, "We're clear on how to play this, right?"

But there wasn't time to go over it. The office door opened and Sergeant Howard motioned them inside. Cloaked in uncertainty, Street followed Gamble in.

Captain Fuller sat as his desk, frowning at a handful of reports. Lieutenant Velasquez and Sergeant Howard flanked the desk, both in a tense mood. Street and Gamble came in side by side and stayed that way.

Fuller made no polite hello or welcome or anything. He flicked his hard eyes up at them.

"It's simple," he said bluntly. "You were ordered to hold. You moved in anyways. Disregarding a direct order from your lieutenant."

Street swallowed a lump and started to answer, but Gamble beat him to it.

"Respectfully, sir," Gamble began, but his tone was not respectful at all, "we don't have time to send a memo up the chain of command before every move we make."

"There was a gunman about to put a bullet into a hostage's head," Street supported.

The captain wasn't fooled. "You didn't know that when you went charging in, though, did you?"

His arm against Street's, Gamble tensed. "That woman's alive because of what we did."

"Alive and suing the city for millions! Chief says if he's got to pay, someone else does too. It sure as hell's not going to be me!"

Gamble's temperature went up another degree. "We get two seconds to make a decision, and you guys get two months to tear it apart and sell us out to the chief?"

"S.W.A.T. means Special Weapons and Tactics," Lieutenant Velasquez broke in. "Where were your tactics out there?"

"Saving a woman from getting shot," Street snapped, "that's where."

"Every cop in this building," Gamble added, "thinks we did the right thing."

Fuller's face reddened. "Sometimes doing the right thing isn't doing the right thing. You disobeyed a direct order. End of story."

But it wasn't the end. The captain paused, then finished.

"You're both off S.W.A.T.," he said.

"Captain—" Velasquez turned. "They're two of our best officers!"

Well, at least the captain hadn't discussed this decision for hours, with everybody, which would've stunk.

Fuller looked at him. "I'm not sticking them back out in the field after that stunt."

"Since when is saving lives considered to be a goddamned stunt?" Gamble demanded—as if he really wanted an answer.

Fuller wasn't in any mood to be queried. "We

may have trained you to be a badass, but that hot-head temper and disregard for the rules that keeps landing you here—that's all *you*."

"Stick 'em somewhere," Velasquez spoke up again. "Just not in the field."

Street felt as if there were an orange stuck in the back of his mouth. He couldn't speak. Before him, the captain considered his fate and Gamble's.

Gamble was quaking inside his skin. Street could sense it without even looking.

"Put 'em on desk duty," the captain said, "till the dust settles. Let them work the cage or something."

"This is total bullshit," Gamble rumbled.

"Really?" Fuller looked up. "You should consider yourself lucky that Lieutenant Velasquez is sticking up for you."

"I'm lucky I don't have to work for an asshole like you anymore."

Gamble's words took Street by the soul. What'd he say?

Fuller pressed back so far that his chair squeaked with strain. He dumped the paperwork onto the desk in front of him. "Easy enough."

Gamble turned on a heel. "Come on," he said to Street.

"Officer Street, you stay," the captain snapped.

Street halted where he stood, caught between the order that meant his career and the friend who had helped make it.

Gamble paused at the door, waiting for him.

This was it. This was the fear that had been cooking under the surface. Street didn't really care about the media or the politicians or talk shows or even the captain's opinion. Even deeper down, he'd known Gamble was on a short string, chewed out one too many times for acting on the instincts that had gotten them both into S.W.A.T. in the first place. They were elite police officers with special training because they had special talents. Gamble's buried rage was the foundation of his great talent. He took right and wrong literally, with very sharp lines.

He was insulted. He should be.

Street held his ground. Somebody had to. This couldn't be it! How do you walk out on your perfect life?

He had orders—*Officer Street, you stay.*

Brian?

Gamble paused at the door. His dark eyes changed. He no longer paid attention to the captain, the sergeant, the lieutenant. His whole mind was on Jim Street. *This is a test. You gonna pass? Partner?*

Then he was gone—just like that. Just walked away. The *tup-tup* of his boots on the hallway linoleum were like little arrows thumping into Street's chest.

Captain Fuller picked up the incident reports again and rifled through them. "According to witness statements," he went on, "you were set up on the other side of the room when Gamble fired."

Street choked out a response. "Yes, sir."

"If Gamble had to fire through the hostage, your angle must have been a clean shot. Right?"

This time Street didn't want to answer, to agree. He would be signing the bottom line on Gamble's career.

So he didn't answer. Silence did the dirty work.

Fuller looked at Velasquez and Howard. "Give Officer Street and me a minute."

Velasquez left the room first, almost anxiously. The sergeant hesitated, but then followed.

When Street was the only one left, Captain Fuller lowered his voice. "Gamble's a bad influence on the rest of the team."

A bad influence on me, you mean.

"Unlike him, you still have a future here," the captain went on, as if Street had answered with some kind of agreement. "I'm going to give you a chance to save your ass. Go on record you had a clean shot and Gamble acted recklessly. I'll have you back on S.W.A.T. tomorrow morning."

Back on, back on, back on S.W.A.T. You can get back on—it'll be like nothing happened. They'll back up the move. They'll smooth things over.

Brian—

"I . . ." He started to speak. Had he actually made a noise yet, or was it he just imagining it?

The captain waited while Street made the decision of a lifetime.

"I wish . . . I could help you, sir," he forced out. "But I was still moving into position. Gamble took the only shot that would've saved the hostage."

Fuller leaned back again and scowled at the pile of manure Street had just dumped on his desk. The wall went up.

"Fine," Fuller said flatly. "Starting tomorrow, you're off S.W.A.T. and in the cage."

Street heard a locker door slam shut as he entered the locker room and knew instinctively it was Gamble. He found his partner in civvies, with his gear packed into a small duffel. Self-conscious that he was still in uniform, Street approached slowly, leaving a little distance between them. It was a psychological cushion, but not enough. Street felt light-headed.

"Good," Gamble said simply, right away. "Let's get the hell out of here."

"I'm staying." Seemed better just to say it right out.

Gamble blinked. "After that?"

Street flapped a hand. "A couple of months, Fuller'll find some new asses to chew out and we'll be back on the team."

"Fuller's the cockroach of the department," Gamble protested bitterly. "He doesn't die, he doesn't leave, and he doesn't give second chances."

Street steeled himself to make a good case. "I'm not gonna piss away all the work we did to get here."

"Piss what away? The cage? Face it! It's over." Gamble seized his duffel bag and stepped over the bench. "You walking out of here with me? Or not?"

But Street's decision had been made. He wanted a future as a S.W.A.T. cop, not an ex-cop. Gamble had talked about a thousand other dreams, but Street had only had one. Maybe Gamble hadn't noticed all the conversations they'd had, thinking and talking and planning wild adventures all over the world. Maybe he'd never noticed that Street just nodded a lot and said, "Yeah, that'd be cool," but he never really said he wanted anything other than what he had.

Gamble might be right. Once off the squad, the way back was long and twisted. Should they strike off on some wild adventure? Without uniforms? No badge? Street couldn't see himself that way. Gamble had lots of talents. Street had only one.

Gamble glared at him. All the affection was gone from his eyes. Whatever they had shared together, today they shared nothing.

"A real partner," he said, "I wouldn't even have to ask."

Suddenly Street was angry. "A *real* partner would step up to what he did in the bank."

"I saved a hostage."

"You disobeyed the hold. Took my shot. Left me wide open!"

"That what you just told Fuller?" Gamble assumed. "You rat me out, cut a deal to get back on the team?"

"God, you can be a real asshole sometimes."

"I'm the asshole who always had your back!"

"And how many times did I cover up for one of your goddamn stunts!"

Oh, this was going just great.

Gamble pulled his shield from his pocket. "Your badge is so goddamned important to you, take mine too."

The bit of metal, so important, struck Street in the chest. Street let it fall and clatter to the locker room floor.

"You gotta throw harder than that if you want to get my attention."

"You just picked a paycheck over me, bro," Gamble warned.

"You're picking yourself over everything else."

"You want to stick around to be Fuller's water boy, be my guest."

Their friendship, and it had been a good one, was crumbling before Jim Street's eyes. Should he go mild, maybe? Plead for more time? Tell Gamble that he hadn't sold him out?

What did it say about them that Gamble could even imagine he'd been sold out in the first place? There was no going back on that one, no point reliving it. No matter how he explained, he wouldn't sound good.

Street felt his arms tingle like some kind of alarm. The friendship broke out of its cage, seized up, and cracked between them, then crumbled at their feet. Just like that. How many years? How many crises? Done? Months of working so closely that people thought they were each other's shadow, of perfect timing, singular goals—

Give it up? Venture out into the world, work for

hire, become mercenaries, hook up to foreign governments, maybe eventually get courted by their own . . .

Trouble was, he *could* imagine it.

They had always wanted the same things. Except Street wanted them in a happy, looking-forward way, and Gamble wanted them in a gimme-what-I-deserve way.

So what? As long as they reached their goals?

But that was the problem, wasn't it? The goals had just separated, as if two currents had come under them and carried them apart, farther and farther by the second.

Sometimes mirrors just break.

"Partners for five years, this is how you want to end it?"

Gamble's eyes turned icy. "You ended it by selling me out to the brass."

"I never realized till now how full of shit you are."

"Fuck you," Gamble said. "And S.W.A.T."

He surprised Street—maybe even surprised himself—by grabbing his yesterday-friend and slamming him back against the floor-length mirror on the locker room wall. Street felt the blow before he had a chance to react. Any other time Gamble would've moved differently, pulled his punch, but today he went ahead and played his advantage.

Instinct took over. Street went ahead and planed his foot, keeping himself from stumbling backward, inviting Gamble to hit him again if that would help.

But Gamble made a wraithlike tower only steps away, his face darkened with anger, eyes forgetful of all they had been through. He was a wounded man who no longer felt pain because his mind was clouded over.

Street tried to put distance between them. Just a few steps, as agony poured through his upper body just from the muscle reaction of being hit.

Suddenly his eyes were blurred, then cleared, and the back of his head ached sharply. The insult burned in his brain.

As Gamble backed away, Street put his hand to his head. It came away bloody. His skull buzzed as if in a frying pan.

He stared at his hand, at the blood, as if it were red ink on a map, drawing their futures in two completely different directions.

3

SURF WAS UP. AH, CALIFORNIA.

The summer months were in full swing and so were the Pacific waves, sweeping in from the north Alaskan seas, still carrying that brisk chill from a few feet under the sun-warmed surface. When the waves rolled into whitecaps, the bathwater on top would be toweled under, and the fresh clear water from the Arctic would turn up, just holding enough cold to make a surfer feel important and seriously awake.

The cold waves were the best ones, Street had always thought. Everybody had a surf philosophy. His was the cold rush. Cleared his head every time. He always went for the coldest, highest curls while everybody else was waiting for the predictable and warm ones.

He rode in toward shore on the tip of a roaring tongue of water, his tanned skin red from the chill, tattoos on his shoulders proclaiming his reckless bachelor life as the muscles worked furiously to stay on top of the board, on top of the tongue. Air blasted at his longish hair. He needed a haircut. Somehow he always needed a haircut, like that guy on *Miami Vice* somehow always needed a shave but never had a beard. There was an art to it. Street figured he had accidentally stumbled on the just-right formula. Hack the ends of the hair off yourself once a month, using a bathroom mirror and a hand mirror, and don't pay all that much attention.

Hell, he had that almost-beard too. He felt as if the time on top of the wave was his only real life. The rest was motions, just motions, empty.

He plowed through a group of other surfers who were sitting on their boards, waiting out the really dangerous wave. Their faces were pasted with shock as he came through on death's own finger. He was crazy, they thought, nobody with a brain would try this wave in this thin-aired weather. The pressure could dissolve under him and he'd take a fifty-foot fall straight down. It was a neck breaker. What was the idea of this sport, anyway? Challenge or suicide? Most people learned the difference early, long before they got to Street's level of skill.

Who cared what they thought?

Oh—now he got it. They were afraid he'd land on them. That must be it.

Well, stay safe, guys. See ya on shore.

On the shore he went through a series of empty motions that brought him back to his daily life, or at least the rest of his day. *Life* wasn't exactly the word for it.

Running. Pavement slapped under his feet, over and over, and his dog, Chopper, jogging alongside him, faithful as a shadow. This good pair of distance runners had been worth the scratch. Anybody who paid that much for a pair of shoes must be serious.

Street gave himself three more compliments as a bribe to increase speed during the last quarter mile. Before him a row of parked cars provided a jagged test range, and he made a mental coin flip before dodging to the right instead of the left. The last four days it had been left. The dog was completely taken off guard. Good sign. Dogs were hard to trick on the run. This was like playing tic-tac-toe with himself, but what the heck. Today there was a great obstacle—an SUV towing a horse trailer. He went right between the two without touching.

The trailer rocked a little as he surprised the slumbering animal inside, but in an instant Street was another ten cars down the row, picking and choosing as he dodged, zigged, and jumped between them in the most complex way possible. Every day the obstacle course was different, just because so many varieties of vehicles came and went from this city lot. Street couldn't have been half as creative if he'd tried to design a course himself.

Besides, "real" was a better test. When it counted, it would be real.

Cars, pickups, motorcycles, RVs of every class, vans, bikes, trucks that carried glass, liquid, animals, wood, houses—yesterday he'd hurdled a hearse. Probably didn't wake anybody up, though.

The living, however, must be wondering why tread marks ended up on their bumpers. The idea was *not* to leave any, but nobody's perfect.

Tucking his right shoulder, he rolled under a flatbed and tried to touch ground with the narrowest part of his hip. Satisfied, he flipped up on the other side and never lost stride, but made a little note to lay the upper leg out longer next time, then pivot up on that toe. Might work.

He ran everywhere. He hadn't had his car out of the garage for months. Six months. It reminded him of Brian. They used to drive everywhere together. Now he just didn't want to get in it unless he really, really had to.

He liked having his dog run with him. Chopper wasn't much for conversation, but he could go for miles before his tongue started to hang out. Of course, keeping up with Street wasn't much of a challenge when he was wearing full police gear and a backpack and police boots. Had to train to run the hard way, after all. How often did a cop end up chasing a perp while wearing jogging shorts and a tank?

In fact, today for the first time he and Chopper overtook that buff jogger from down the street, the guy with the Nikes and shorts. *Yeah, boy.*

Of course, when it came down to the punching bag on Street's little balcony outside his apartment, Chopper pretty much just watched in doggy amazement at why anybody, human or otherwise, would stand there for an hour hitting a stuffed opponent. The dog would look once in a while at his stuffed football doggy toy, wondering whether he should be doing the same thing, but then he'd give up and just lick the beach sand off his paws for a while.

But jogging was better than sitting inside. With *her*.

When had the girl he had loved so much and sweated over and lusted for turned into just *her*?

Good thing they hadn't gotten engaged. Damn good thing. Funny how relationships could change, swing such a wide arch. Him and her, him and Brian . . . him and S.W.A.T.

This was life? A maniac in incredible condition, sweat flying off his lean arms, and nothing to do with it. He wasn't a cop. He was just still on the force, whatever that meant to somebody who had once been S.W.A.T.

How do you go down from that? How do you climb down without bruising your—just about everything?

Life in the cage. In more than one way.

The cage. In the Metro building of the L.A.P.D., Street had become the man in the cage, the one the first shift was used to seeing in there. It had taken a good two months before the looks of pained pity started to go away, or at least his fellow officers got control over them. He did his job like a trooper, determined to show them all that he was a cop whether he was in the cage or behind an M-16, and he could do it all cheerfully. Word would get around, back to Captain Fuller and Lieutenant Velasquez that Jim Street was determined to do the best job possible, even if he were sweeping a floor. He would sweep the floor better than anybody else and earn the next step up. He could eat his pride and digest it too.

That was the great plan. After six months the greatness of it was wearing thin. He was smiling less. The smiles were forced. The jokes were sour now. The pity from his fellow officers was like a continuous burn. He'd rather have the jokes.

Now they didn't say much of anything to him, unless he started the conversation. Then they got away as quickly as they could. Life in the cage.

He and Chopper skirted the corner of the L.A.P.D. Central Station's concrete fortress wall. Keeping the tempo of his stride, he flashed his ID at the guards, who knew him anyway, then vaulted the concrete barriers without slowing down, and he was inside. He closed his eyes and bore left, counting footsteps. When the temperature changed, he knew he'd counted right and gotten the length of strides just right too. First time this week.

When he opened his eyes, they were partly adjusted and he could see fairly well despite having run in sunlight until now. The dark maw of the garage swallowed him and Chopper.

Once inside, he shivered off the rush of cool air laced with a scent of lubricants, gasoline, exhaust, and rubber. The temper of the vehicles changed too. Darker, less jazzy, no markings, thicker-bodied, with blackwalls. Suburbans, trucks, unmarked cars, and even cars pretending to be junkers provided an armada at the ready. Not the vehicles a teenager really wanted, and sometimes Street wondered if that might be the one big difference between men and boys.

Men still needed toys, but the toys were serious.

These were mobile armories, surveillance posts, and rolling command centers, standing at the rest like guards waiting for the signal to spring. Which ones would roll today? Without him?

Street played the mental game as he ran deeper into the garage and into the equipment cage where his run would have to end. Surrounded not by a forest of helmets, radios, flak vests, body armor, belts, holsters, boots, flashbang grenades, weaponry, and tools of every description, he jogged in place for a few seconds and checked his time.

Four seconds faster than yesterday, but ten slower than the day before. He got water for Chopper, then arranged for the morning patrol to drop his dog back off at his own place, as usual. Chopper was sort of a quasi-K-9 corps, and everybody on the force liked and accepted him, so it was no big deal to give him a lift.

During his shower he went over the route in his mind and decided where to speed up. Maybe that rock garden next to the new condo complex. The shower made him smell better, but he was still flushed when he came back to the cage in uniform. The uniform never felt right. Too comfortable. Too office. Where the hell was his Thermos?

A couple of seconds later he'd found it and got after the morning ritual of cream, sugar, a fistful of vitamins, some protein powder, a good long shake, and a daily reminder to buy a blender. No putting it off . . . time to sit at the . . . the . . . desk. Desk, okay?

Here he was again today, in the cage, distributing equipment to men who should be proud of him and in awe of him for his skills. He had the skills, clearly, but wasn't allowed to use them. Skill meant nothing without the wisdom to use them properly. At least, that was the philosophy. Probably right. He'd lied his way around it. He'd protected Gamble, and it hadn't worked. Now he was stuck with his lie, and everybody knew he'd been lying. Only Gamble didn't know.

He settled into his job and deliberately turned his back on the shrine of shooting trophies, S.W.A.T. Olympic trophies, and photos of better days. There was even one left of him and Gamble. He's never had the heart to toss it, and every morning it pinched a little.

A thunder of activity shook him from what might have been a wash of reverie and unhappiness. He flinched and looked up at a herd of S.W.A.T. cops in crisp fatigues as they stampeded out of the briefing room across from his cage. He knew a lot of guys on the force wondered why he wanted this assignment, tormenting himself every day with S.W.A.T. equipment, S.W.A.T. officers, S.W.A.T. memorabilia, S.W.A.T. you name it.

He straightened his shoulders and put down his drink as two of the young S.W.A.T. team members crossed toward the equipment cage. Boxer was a little overweight, but in all the right places, a go-with-the-flow type with perpetual five-o'clock shadow—how he got that at nine in the morning was anybody's guess—and T.J. was an arrogant perfectionist with the hair and teeth of a teen idol. They didn't exactly make Street nervous, though he became more aware of his posture for a few seconds.

By the time the two cops got to his gate, Street had their ammo boxes on his counter and ready.

"Hey, Boxer," he greeted.

"Morning, Jim. How's my sister?"

"She wasn't up yet when I left," Street said, deliberately evasive. "I heard a new crew is manning up."

"I heard we're getting a raise," T.J. countered, "but I don't see it happening. You've been around too long to listen to rumors."

Despite the scolding, Street dredged up a grin. "Come on, I'll find out anyway when the captain has me outfit them. I hear they're going to add a six-man element to the duty rotation."

"No comment," Boxer said.

The meaning of that was pretty clear. No speaking of departmental details to the trigger-happy has-been who was bucking for a comeback shot.

Street clamped his mouth shut on any more questions. T.J. and Boxer grabbed their ammo and evaporated toward one of the Suburbans before they had to exchange any more words with Street about why he, out of six hundred highly qualified badass applicants, would have any more chance of getting back on Special Weapons and Tactics. He made them uneasy, but he didn't care.

Back to the same old, same old. Fill in the blank for whatever came after, and it was still old. The crowded station was a workaday place where nobody cared about frills, a place where generations of cops had come to toughen up, mostly men and women who couldn't quite decide whether they really wanted to retire someday or go down in the line of duty and never see eternity coming. An hour later Street was still here at the gate, but now he was watching his assistant, Officer Gus Leonardson, finish his second Dr Pepper. Joy.

"You're a little too attached to that soda, Gus," Street said, forcing an end to the silence that had settled in after the garage emptied of duty officers out on their rounds.

"Love this stuff," the thirty-something patrolman said. "The wife would have my behind if she busted me sucking this down."

"Why's that? She a Mr. Pibb fan?"

"You know the deal, Jim. When we got married, I converted to Mormonism. We can't consume anything that alters our state of mind. We treat our bodies with respect."

Street picked at his paperwork, more aware of the ten S.W.A.T. officers being called to roll way over there. They ignored him in an almost professional manner, but he could tell his eyes made them aware of themselves. What the hell. He'd been there. He'd be back. Let them be uneasy.

"And I treat mine like an amusement park," he drawled. "It's the differences that make this country great."

He was very different now from the surfer, or the guy with the punching bag and the dog, or any of his other personae. He was cleaned up, combed, shaved, and buttoned down. He'd be on duty for the next four days, twelve-hour shifts. Then the scruffy off-duty jerk would surface again. For now, he was sweeping the floor perfectly.

Oh, great. Here came Boxer again. Another buff thirty, wearing a tight muscle shirt and carrying muddy boots. He tossed the boots onto the counter and bluntly ordered, "I need 'em cleaned by morning."

Luckily, before Street could speak up, Gus Leonardson did. "You were supposed to have your gear in half an hour ago."

Boxer gestured at Street, but did him the indignity of speaking to Leonardson. "Your boy gonna report me to the captain?

"Yeah," Street spoke for himself. "For thinking you look good in that shirt."

After all, he didn't have to kiss *their* butts, exactly, did he? No. Even crow could be eaten with some sauce now and then.

Something about it worked. Boxer actually smiled at him as Street put the boots down on the floor to be cleaned later. Was that respect? Maybe a little?

He was suddenly pleased with himself that his scraping of the bottom was beginning to get some begrudging kind thoughts from cops who had been pretty prickly before. Boxer's smile was a heck of a checkmark.

"Uh-oh," Boxer said then, his attention turned in another direction. He was looking out at the Metro garage, where a Crown Victoria had just come to a stop.

"Oh, shit!" Gus said. "It's Hondo!"

They watched as a uniformed officer who had been driving the car rushed around to open the big car's passenger door, but then somebody stopped him. What came out of the car first was a gun—an M-4 . . . a chopped M-16. No shit, for sure. Then a duffel bag. The car's passenger then stepped out, doing his carrying for himself.

He was a very bad dude, or thought he was, and came out clean, crisp, starched, and serious.

Street frowned in annoyance.

The new man crossed to the cage. He was big, strong, uninterested in those around him, and he lay his weapon on the counter as if he did it every day.

"What do you need?" Street asked blandly.

Leonardson, though, was positively in hero-worship mode. "Sergeant Hondo . . . you're back!"

The man called Hondo gave him a glance, but not much of one. "Well, Gus, you're either S.W.A.T. or you're not."

"Yes, sir! What do you need?"

"A little tune-up. Please don't touch the sights. I've made some modifications."

Street eyed the weapon. "To the trigger too."

"Right."

"We'll leave them intact."

"I need it by tomorrow."

"Can do, Sergeant!" Gus piped up.

Street looked at his watch as Sergeant Daniel "Hondo" Harrelson crossed over to the roll call and made his presence known. "Gosh, Gus, I've never seen you move so fast." He looked at the weapon again. "Is that a woody?"

"Heck, yeah! That's Hondo. He's old-school S.W.A.T. The gold standard of ass-kicking. Sorry, butt-kicking. Fuller forced him out a couple of years ago. Guess he's back."

Street took Hondo's M-4 and began stripping it. "Well, now I'm the one with the woody."

But inside he was glowing. He had just seen proof, the first, that there was a way back onto the team, by God. If Hondo could find it, then so could James W. Street, by God, by God.

So how could he get as special as Hondo?

There was a way.

He had to find it.

By God.

"You get lost or something?"

Greg Velasquez sat at his desk and read the newspaper, or pretended to. The *L.A. Times*. He blinked up at the knock on his door and worked pretty damned hard at not looking surprised. Oh, hell, he just couldn't do it!

He tossed the paper down and stood up when Hondo laughed at his remark.

"I know your sense of direction is for shit, but Jesus!" Velasquez bellowed. "Three years!"

"Barely through your door and already you're busting my balls!" Hondo roared, and stuck out his hand.

Velasquez took the hand—still strong—and let himself be pulled into a hug. "It's good to have you back! How's your swing coming along? You fix that slice yet?"

"Put up some money and find out."

"Something tells me I can't afford to."

"What in Christ is this?" Hondo broke the contact, scooped up the *L.A. Times*, and glared at the headline.

L.A.P.D. PERCEIVED AT ALL-TIME LOW.

"A weeklong series," Velasquez explained. "Attacking us from top to bottom. Recruitment is down eighteen percent. Violent crime is up twelve."

"And it's all S.W.A.T.'s fault, right?"

"No, the Chief's been pretty fair about blaming everyone. But he wants an end to these bad headlines."

They slumped into the two chairs, one behind the desk and one in front, but they were still shaking hands in their minds.

"I don't work for the papers," Hondo bolted.

Velasquez eyed him. "He wants some of the old warhorses to help restore the luster."

"Old? I know you ain't talking about me."

"You better shake off that three-year rust from Rampart," Velasquez said with a lilt. "I'm throwing you into the shit right away!"

"Sooner, the better."

That was just what Velasquez wanted to hear. He had only half expected to hear it. Hell, he hadn't exactly been sure Hondo would actually come back, after the crap he'd been dealt by Fuller three years ago.

Velasquez leaned forward with both elbows on his desk and talked serious. "Put together a young kick-ass element for me, Dan. You select them. You train them. You mold them—"

"Wait! You're not talking about giving me five pups out of the gate!"

"Shit, no!"

"—'cause I didn't come back to wipe noses."

"You worked with T.J. and Boxer back at Southwest. You up for supervising them here?"

"You read my mind, Greg."

"Then all you have to do is find three fresh

ones. Only catch is Fuller's got to approve the three."

Hondo leaned back till the chair squawked. "And what did Fuller say when he heard Chief was bringing me back?"

Velasquez pressed his lips tight, because he wasn't sure whether he'd laugh or cry.

"Hasn't stopped swearing since," he said.

4

She was carrying a box toward the door. He had to step aside for her, but she didn't continue past him. She was surprised. Hadn't expected to see him here right now. Hoped for a clean escape, probably. Wrecked that.

Lara was sexy in a life's-too-short kind of way. Life's too short for commitment, marriage, big talk, small talk, or talk at all. Maybe that was the problem.

"What's Boxer's truck doing outside?" Street asked her, as if he didn't know. "We having a garage sale I don't know about?"

"You weren't supposed to be home for an hour," she said. Her voice was strained, thin. There was sadness, but somehow no regret at all. Weren't they the same sometimes? Shouldn't they be the same today?

"Sorry to screw up your getaway." Oops—now he'd done it himself. He'd mixed sincerity with resentment. Weird. Talents he didn't even know he had.

She pulled the box tight to her chest and stood back on a heel. "Look . . . let's not make this a thing. We've both known it was coming. It's not like we got into this to get married. You've changed since . . ."

Then she stopped, tried to think of the right thing to say, and Street just watched her eyes in a way he probably should've watched them a long time ago.

"Look," she began again, as if she hadn't said the other part, "while it was good, it was great. That's something, isn't it?"

Apparently she wasn't looking for a real answer. He didn't even try.

She leaned up a little and kissed him, one of those kisses you don't really like to get. Her hair was freshly scented with Pantene and her tanned skin warm. She left a haze of hunger and a kind of lover's pity clinging to him when she escaped out the door of his apartment.

Jim Street stood there with his own jogging sweat putting off a smolder. He looked at the apartment. Sparse furniture, a TV, the punching bag on the balcony, a spiffy-clean kitchen—she'd done that before she left. Girl thing.

Well . . . woman thing. She'd grown up.

He hadn't changed. She had. He should have, but he hadn't.

Over in the corner by the window, Chopper lay on his blanket with a half-chewed rawhide bone, but he wasn't playing with the bone. He was just watching Street. At least the dog was staying put. At least Street had something left of the better life from six months ago.

Was it only six months?

"I've got to get out," he mourned. "I gotta get out of the cage."

Twenty-five S.W.A.T. cops, a couple of sergeants, Lieutenant Velasquez on the podium, reading his notes.

Hondo strode in but hung back. He knew he had a reputation and didn't want to flag it around, or seem to be doing that. Somebody else would do it for him, he hoped in the right amount to get done what he needed to do. Things were already pretty much going his way. The L.A.P.D. needed to turn the clock both back and forward at the same time. Back to a tougher, leaner department, forward to something that could handle the heightened stress in the city these days, but do it clean, like the old days.

He smiled at himself, just a little. "Old" days? Wasn't all that long ago, but it seemed like a lifetime. All these new men were fresh-faced and strong, old enough to have sense and young enough to use it. He knew some of them, but by far most of the twenty-five were a newer breed. Several of the men he had known in S.W.A.T. had moved on to training and command positions in other police forces around the country, valued for their in-the-fire experience in Greater Los Angeles, which they could take to hot spots in Detroit, Baltimore, Cleveland, Orlando, you name it. He knew, because he'd checked.

He stayed back, quiet. No one had noticed him yet, including—he thought—Velasquez at the podium. There was a certain curiosity about what would be said. He knew what they were talking about.

"The two guys with the lowest shooting scores tomorrow get to pick up everybody else's brass." Greg Velasquez seemed to be enjoying himself, putting on the air of a big bear on the prowl. When he looked up from the notes in his hand, he saw Hondo loitering in the back of the room, shimmied up against a United States flag on a stand.

Suddenly self-conscious, Hondo shifted just enough to put a foot between himself and the flag, out of respect. Wouldn't look good if they got the idea he thought he was some kind of hero who had the right to stand so close.

Velasquez paused, but only an instant.

"Gentlemen, our new Seventy-David has just made his first stealth entry. If you don't know him, you've probably heard of him. Sergeant Dan 'Hondo' Harrelson."

All faces turned. Through his dark skin Hondo felt his cheeks flush. *Please let the complexion hide it—*

Most of the expressions seemed favorable. Whatever the rumors were, seemed the word was good about him. He got a quiver at the idea of living up to what he saw in these men's eyes.

Men and women. *I'll be damned, there are a couple of girls out there.*

"Hondo worked S.W.A.T. twelve years," Velasquez filled in grandly, "and defected to Rampart to earn his stripes, where he straightened things out and pushed the P.M. watch to their best ratings reports ever. Hondo's won the medal twice and has a handful of bravery stars to boot. He will outrun, outfight and outshoot, and outpaperwork all of you."

T. J. McCabe piped up as if he'd been fired out of a cannon. "Outshoot? Lieutenant, come on! You still inhaling that marijuana burning we supervised yesterday?"

"I'm just commentating."

"Twenty bucks says otherwise."

Boxer quickly said, "I'll cover ten of that."

Now there were a lot of smiles out there, and a couple of red faces, like they might be all charged up but also embarrassed. Hondo wished Velasquez hadn't thrown that out there.

"Gambling's not allowed. And I'll cover the other ten." Velasquez seemed to realize he'd made a mistake that might cause Hondo some embarrassment, or at least stir up trouble that might have been avoided. "Anything you want to say to the troops, Hondo?"

Hondo cleared his throat, but not loudly enough for anybody else to notice.

"As a matter of fact, there is." He held his ground, didn't move forward. This was not the time for a showful stride. "Coming back to S.W.A.T., I do have one pressing concern. And quite frankly, it almost kept me from accepting this promotion." He turned and leveled a severe glower onto the infamous Sergeant Howard, who had been sitting quietly until now. "Sergeant Howard, when you're in the locker room, do you still blow-dry your hair naked, in front of the mirror?"

The room broke into laughter. Boxer bellowed, "After every workout!"

Only Sergeant Howard avoided cracking up. There was way, way too much truth going on in here today.

"That shit has got to stop if we're gonna turn this department around!" Hondo crowed. He let his own smile show where he was coming from. He wanted them to like him, not just respect him. He wanted the command officers on a new kind of level with the uniformed men. When the laughter finally drifted down some, he said, "On a serious note, I'm honored to be here. I don't know you all personally, but you wear the uniform and that means I'd take a bullet for every one of you. Except for you, T.J."

A little more laughter. Just enough. So far, so good.

"All right," Greg Velasquez interrupted. "Let's catch some bad guys."

While Jim Street reassembled the M-4 carbine, using a series of special gunsmithing tools he'd collected in his own spare time, Gus Leonardson rumbled around the other side of the cage, storing and shifting and stacking. When Gus tripped over something that made a familiar ring, he said, "I'm gonna throw this thing out."

Street twisted around and warned, "You do and you die. Every S.W.A.T. team in the world's going to have one of those some day."

"It's fifty pounds of scrap metal!"

"Say you got some crazy barricaded in a house," Street explained. "Just chain it to the back of a truck, shove this end right through the wall"—he turned a little more and pointed at the parts of the goofy looking contraption—"these rods spring out like a fishhook. Your partner guns the truck . . . takes the whole wall with him."

"Then *you* walk in and surprise the bad guy?"

Street gave him a bitter glare with a touch of an oath in it. "I call it the 'Key to the City.' Patent pending."

"Really?" But it wasn't Gus who said that—it was Hondo. When had he come up to the cage?

Street looked up at him. "No, but it sounds good." He rubbed a fingerprint off the gleaming M-4 and handed it to Hondo, deliberately not saying anything else.

Hondo took the road-worn weapon and inspected it the way a man intimately knows his own right arm. "Took the rattle out of the receiver . . . smoothed up the trigger . . . new buffer . . . gas rings . . . cleaned the gas tube . . . and . . . new batteries and bulbs."

"Well, Gus worships you, so I decided to do it right." Street bounced a vengeful grin off Gus, who squirmed with discomfort.

"Surprised you didn't starch the sling," Hondo added.

Street shrugged, then dared one step over the line. "You want me to show you how to shoot it? I'm here all week, nine to five."

Hondo paused, glaring at him. Was it a glare of intrigue? After all, nobody else in the department would've had the gall to say something like that. Street was counting on gall to get him through. Get him back in. It was all he had.

"Thanks," Hondo drawled. Then he turned and strode off to join T.J. and Boxer at the long black S.W.A.T. Suburban, parked on the far side of the Metro garage. Street watched them go, and wondered whether he had planted the right kind of seed—or just pissed in the dirt.

Dan Harrelson had stopped thinking of himself as "Dan" about twenty years ago. Half the time, if somebody called him Dan, he didn't even think to answer. He'd been stuck with "Hondo" since the Marine Corps. Kind of liked it now, though he hadn't at first. He didn't even really know where it'd come from. Some punk had started calling him that, and it stuck. At first he'd fought it some, but then he got to like the idea of a nickname. It was convenient cover sometimes, he'd learned. It also carried a sort of mystique that he could use to his advantage. Like Batman.

He sat in his favorite chair, on the deck of his Los Feliz home, and gazed out at the lights of nighttime L.A. as he sipped on a bottle of beer and drowned the latest bite of his corned beef and romaine sandwich. A little grittier than he liked.

The night air was pretty fresh, considering, and the night absolutely—*absolutely*—quiet. There was no traffic noise, no airplanes, no wind. Perfect. His little floor lamp here was the only light, other than stars and a sliver of moon. He would've turned out the light except for having to read these files. Profiles, really, of the men from which he would choose his S.W.A.T. team that would turn L.A. around.

Big ideas, small steps. These were the first steps—the unglamorous task of picking through the bios and service records of twenty-five potential special servicemen.

He flinched when a bush rustled, but it was only a deer poking along the edge of his property. The delicate prey animal seemed both in and out of place here. The scruffy woodlands were just right for wildlife, but the city beyond was a relentless reminder of harsh truths of civilization in Southern California.

"Get off my damn property," Hondo grumbled. "Gonna eat my geraniums."

The deer didn't move, except to flick its ears toward him. Its big eyes caught the glint of moonlight, and its hide, probably a nice moccasin brown, looked silver right now.

Hondo felt himself soften some. "We got coyotes up here," he warned. "You better watch out for those sneaky bastards, you hear?"

The deer flicked again, then, as if it understood him, bolted back into the woods. Smart kid.

Hondo sucked another gulp of beer and picked up the next file. Yeah, this one. He'd asked for it special. Velasquez had had a gleam in his eye when he handed it to him. Said something about Fuller, but Hondo couldn't remember the mutter.

Was this another of Fuller's guillotined former specialists? Trouble was probably this guy's middle name. Same as Hondo's. Dan Hondo Trouble Get the Hell off My Force Harrelson.

So this guy . . . James Wilson Trouble Get the Hell Out Street.

Street? This was a name? Street, on the streets. Hit the street, Street.

Silly. Or was it fate? Soldiers, cops, and gang members tended to give each other funky nicknames, but apparently this was this guy's actual name. The smart-ass in the cage. How long had he been in there?

Hondo opened the file and started reading, this one with a little special interest. He read for ten minutes, then reread for another five.

Then he picked up the cell phone on the redwood table beside him and punched in the new speed-dial number he'd just fed into the system today.

"Greg? Yeah, so what? You don't need no beauty

sleep. Wake up and talk to me. I wanna talk to you about this one guy."

Pok pok pok pok pok pok pok

Rapid fire. The kind of even shooting that only goes on in a controlled setting. The kind other officers watch while it's going on, to measure against their own.

Hondo stood slightly turned to one side, bracing his shooting hand with his other wrist, popping off the row of ten targets set up way down the range. Beside him the S.W.A.T. cop named T.J. did the same. Their shots echoed each other within milliseconds.

Behind them a cluster of S.W.A.T. officers watched. Hondo knew they had their money on him. He'd knitted that reputation carefully over the years. He wanted respect and a drop or two of fear, and he'd had the recipe to get it. He was big, strong, quiet, old enough to know what he wanted, and young enough to get it. His record was fierce and edgy, just on this side of the right side.

Unfortunately, that meant from time to time living up to the rep. And he slipped. Missed the last target.

T.J. got his, all ten of them.

T.J. turned to the other men and grinned. "How could you ever doubt me?" he chimed.

Velasquez shook his head and growled, "Because *he* used to be the best I ever saw." He glowered at Hondo.

"*Used* to be," Boxer spoke up.

Hondo smiled anyway. He was glad for T.J. He'd seen in McCabe's eyes how much he wanted to make Hondo's team. That meant being able to shoot as well as Hondo. T.J. had just outdone him, and knew he was on. Nobody else had done that.

He smiled again when he realized that T.J. was actually tearing up at his victory. "There's a few people I have to thank," McCabe began, and his words got stronger as he spoke. "My fellow S.W.A.T. officers, for seeing my talent when the bosses didn't . . . my parents, for without them I wouldn't be $120 richer this morning—"

Boxer laughed, and was the first of many to start handing over twenty-dollar bills to the winning bet.

Hondo stuck a hand out to T.J. They might not believe it, but he was reassured to have a team who could match or outdo him. "That's why you're the marksman and I'm the one telling you who to shoot."

And Hondo handed over his own twenty-dollar bill.

Boom boom boom boom boom boom

After a collective flinch—just part of the job— they all turned to look at where the extra shots were coming from. That was no pistol.

It was a shotgun. A specialized, sawed-off street weapon, probably confiscated in a bust.

Oh, yeah, and that one guy was behind the gun. Hit every target at the designated distance too. With a *shotgun*.

He saw something in Street's posture, and something in the faces of the other men. Why was he off by himself? Didn't they want to be around this guy? What was the story behind the story? Hondo had read the file, knew the basic occurrences that had led to this talented cop's ending up in the cage, but what was the real tale? What was the relationship with the abruptly missing Brian Gamble? Two cops that good, with so much intricate timing and perfect match work between them, didn't just say see-ya one day on a whim. Something had cracked. What?

"A hundred bucks," Hondo began, "say that guy hands you your ass."

Boxer bristled. "Are you kidding, Hondo? Come on . . . he's our gun bunny."

"Make it two hundred, then."

"Sure," T.J. took him up. "I got a condo to pay off."

Hondo simply walked over to Street, who was now loading up on ammunition. Nobody else followed.

"Wanna make some extra money?" he asked.

Jim Street offered only the merest of glances. "Not in it for the money."

"How about making me some money, then?" Hondo challenged.

Five minutes later Street and McCabe were set up in competition on the firing line. Street had a .45-caliber handgun, was chewing gum, and had his eyes closed, like he was meditating or something.

Hondo offered him eye and ear protection. "Here. Take my eyes and ears."

"I don't need eyes and ears," Street said. "Don't have 'em on the street."

Hondo smiled, and saw from the corner of his eye that Velasquez was suddenly grinning too. They both liked that. Never mind it was a gutsy one-liner, but it was also true.

T. J. McCabe looked as if he had already spent the money. This was one confident customer. Street didn't have any expression at all as he set his handgun down and picked up an M-4.

Velasquez blew the starting whistle, just a second or two before the men were ready, obviously on purpose. To their credit, both Street and T.J. broke from where they were preparing their weapons and bolted, firing on the run at the rows and rows of disorganized targets set up for just such an exercise. The training, not the bet.

First they shot with M-4s, a furious repetitive rattle so unremitting that it sent shivers up the spines of the observing men. Then they dropped their cover and spat lead with their handguns, so close to each other's movements that either could've been moving next to a mirror. Then something happened.

Street began to pull ahead. To shoot faster by those few milliseconds that, added together, made a big difference. Targets on Street's sight range began to fall faster, faster, then almost in a single sweeping motion. Within moments Street plowed the course flat, while T.J. was playing catch-up. Soon there was only a single gun shooting. Street was already finished.

The other men shifted in astonished discomfort. Only Hondo and Velasquez were not surprised.

Gazing out over the field of destroyed targets, Hondo surveyed his new discovery. Jim Street just stood there, enduring T.J.'s smoldering glare and the uneasy shifting of the other men.

Because he knew.

LOS ANGELES INTERNATIONAL AIRPORT CUSTOMER BAGGAGE CLAIM

Hundreds of passengers streamed from the airport's dozens of corridors, planes, transit offerings, elevators, and terminals. The stream was impressive, rarely slackened, sometimes swelled, and occasionally eased, but never ended. From here and to here, people moved around the world, funneling to millions of private locations in this enormous sprawling city and its many neighboring cities, and from here to almost everywhere else. LAX was in many ways a city on its own, where travelers from anywhere could rest, rush, shop, sleep, wait, eat, get a massage or a haircut, buy new shoes or a belt, or other things, speak or not, be neighborly or not, meet one another, or come to parting moments. This was a place of critical turning points, hopeful beginnings, and sad endings, and it had a thousand stories to tell by the hour, by the day, but it wasn't talking. The many stories would have to tell themselves, one at a time.

Alexander Lupin was one of the stories, one that wasn't going to tell. Lips clamped, he deplaned with a stream of exhausted coach passengers, and he grimaced uneasily at the smell of them. They were the rabble he spent most of his time and money avoiding. Today, though, they were his cover. They served his purpose. A perfectly good reason for them to exist at all. They were nameless, purposeless, and he could never work up a shit about them except on days like this, when he could use them.

He was a plain man, bookish, well dressed, but not up to his usual standard of couture. This was like a costume, this off-the-rack suit. It was a disguise.

There was the immigrations inspector, the ultimate border guard. These American inspectors and customs agents were very careful these days, personifying a loud clang of the barn door. Nothing was as easy as it had been in years past, during which Lupin had built his notorious network. He had no doubt every inspector here knew his real name.

With a glance at the dog team just over there, he calmly handed over his fake passport. Then he fished around in his ugly suit and also handed over his customs declarations.

The immigrations inspector had the usual border guard's sense of humor. He flicked through the passport and papers without looking up at Lupin. "What's the purpose of your visit to the United States?"

"Pleasure," Alex explained, pushing his accent as far as it would go. "I see . . . beach. Hollywood sign."

His light stature once again proved an advantage. He just didn't look like what he was.

And as simply as that, his passport was stamped. ADMITTED.

He was in.

In the bottom of the airport he collected his bags, though he knew he would have to go through yet another inspection. Two customs agents were going to probe his bag, with their latex-covered hands pushing through his personal possessions, his clothing, toiletries . . . the enormous switchblade he always kept with him . . .

"You recognize this?"

Lupin gazed down at the expensive knife, obviously not something your average tourist happened to carry. "Yes . . . father tell me to bring. America dangerous place. True?"

The two agents traded a look.

"Not true," the redheaded one said. "I don't know how you got this through De Gaulle."

"Gift from father," Lupin said quickly. "And gift from his father! Please . . . when I have son, I give to him!"

He made sure his eyes got big and watery. He placed his hand on his heart. Americans would go for that.

The two agents looked at each other again, admired the beautiful workmanship on the knife, clearly an antique, yet in perfect condition, cleaned, oiled and tended with great care. Money could buy that kind of weapon.

The other agent took the knife from the redhead. "Don't bring it back through the airport," he said, placing the knife back into Lupin's travel bag. "Mail it home."

Lupin broke into a stupid grin and snapped the case shut. "Thank you! I will see you!"

He waved at them twice more on his way out of the area. If only he could bottle stupidity like that. He'd be even richer.

A stretch Lincoln Town Car waited outside Bradley Terminal, in a specially licensed parking area. It wasn't really an official parking area, but bribes could talk.

He played his harmless tourist routine until he got to the car, where he ditched the facade along with his travel bag. But he took the knife out first and slipped it into his pocket, where it belonged.

Gift from father. Yeah.

The man behind the wheel made no expressions of any kind, just right for his line of work, as Alex Lupin slumped into the passenger seat. The front seats were better for attracting less attention than a driver and the man being driven. He didn't want to attract attention in this country. Not yet, anyway.

"How was the flight?" G.Q. asked. It was just a nickname, because Lupin didn't want to become familiar with anyone working with him. Their real names were in his database, but he didn't memorize them. This one got his nickname from the rumpled clothes he wore. Somehow G.Q. could put on a suit fresh from the dry cleaners and have it rumpled in ten minutes. Maybe it was his posture. Or his attitude?

"I popped a Valium," Lupin responded dryly, in his usual perfect English. "I hate bumpy planes. Did you get my return ticket and documents?"

"In the glove box. Flight leaves tonight at midnight. In and out."

G.Q. handed Lupin an envelope, which Lupin unzipped with his knife's blade. Inside were a new passport, a wallet full of corresponding fake IDs, including a membership to a video-rental club, and credit cards. And, of course, the plane ticket back home. Business in this silly country would be short, sweet, and effective.

"No one knows I'm here?"

"Just me. Where do you want to go?"

"It's my uncle's birthday. I want to surprise him."

He leaned back in his seat, using the auto-adjust to fix the headrest the way he wanted it to be, and thought about how much he liked surprises.

5

JIM STREET SAT IN THE EQUIPMENT CAGE, WATCHING GUS Leonardson wolf a Big Mac and a Dr Pepper. How could he do that to himself? Never mind the curse of God, how could he do it—just anyway?

"Isn't that eternal damnation you're chowing down there?" he asked, even after he'd sworn to himself that he wouldn't say anything to the would-be converted Mormon.

Gus blinked in a kind of threat that went in both directions. "You can't tell Michelle!"

"Isn't she gonna smell the fries on your breath?"

"Mouthwash. She'll never know."

"Gus," Street said with a tone of significance, "you're cheating on your wife . . . with fast food."

Gus paused between the Big Mac and a fry. He stared down at his food. His beautiful, greasy, salty, soft, carnivorous delight, with no redeeming characteristics and every reason to indulge.

Something changed in his face, his eyes, as the food turned to some kind of emotional poison right while he was watching. Poor Gus—caught between marital and moral commitment and the pure love of grease.

Street held his breath and tried not to grin as Gus muttered, "I know," and kept stuffing his face.

Luckily, Hondo Harrelson came up and interrupted the strained epiphany. Street forgot about Gus and the trials of religion and looked up at the legendary officer who had managed to stir things up without really even trying very hard.

"You got a driver's license, Street?" Hondo asked without a hello or a go to hell or anything.

"Got a library card," Street offered.

"Close enough." Hondo threw him a set of keys. "You're driving me today."

Street didn't move. Hondo walked away.

Gus just looked at Street, baffled. Drive him? *Drive* him? Like Miss Daisy?

After a minute Gus nudged, asking, "You heard the sergeant. . . ."

Street gave him a glare, then got up. "What the hell. That Crown Vic, I s'pose."

"It's on the right. What do you think he—"

"I don't know. Just wants a chauffeur, I guess."

"Yeah. Sure he does, Jim. When your body floats to shore, I'll ID it."

"I got a mole on my butt shaped like Jennifer Lopez's right boob."

"Okay, I, uh—" Gus tried to make a quick response, but suddenly he was laughing and couldn't do it.

Street grinned to hide his nervousness. What *did* Hondo want?

He walked to the Crown Victoria and got in—to find that Hondo was already inside, lounging back in the passenger seat, shuffling through seven or eight personnel files. Street slid into the driver's seat without a word.

This was a dogshit assignment. He'd thought all the rubbing-in was over with months ago. Somebody had it in for him all over again. Why would it be Hondo? Hondo was putting the new hyperteam together, and at first Street had harbored some hopes. He'd done everything he could to impress Hondo, but discovered early that Hondo wasn't one to be impressed. Hondo had been using him for some kind of toy to tease the other men, probably threatened them with bring back the has-beens and never giving them a chance.

Fun, being the stooge.

Street pulled out into the bright California sunshine and had a sudden shiver at how many successful people there were out in the big city, people working at their chosen jobs, or just lucky slobs who ended up in the right place at the right time, talent or not, or those who just happened to sleep in the right beds or crawl into the right hot tubs. He hadn't been willing to do the wrong things nor lucky enough to have the right things fall in front of him. Everything he had, he had because of hard work.

He had lost it all because of the same ethic. Lost

it because he wouldn't turn on Gamble, wouldn't describe the situation to anyone because there was no good way to do that, and therefore even Gamble hadn't believed him.

And because he wouldn't cave to Fuller's pressure. He had stuck out the lowest duty around for a trained S.W.A.T. officer, without failing, without complaint, without quitting. He'd had some idea his stubborn sense of duty and willingness to take all the low roads, endure the ribbings, and do the dirty work would be taken as valuable, or at least laudable.

Still no luck, though. Now he was driving around a guy who was starting to believe his own reputation.

"If you want me to come over and mow your lawn later," he finally said, just to hear a voice, "I'm available, Sergeant."

Ouch. Bad tone of voice.

Then again, what were they going to do? Bust him down even lower?

The voice from the other seat was steady and uncaused. "I'll keep that in mind. And call me Hondo. I did two years in Nam in the Marines. Recon unit. Spent the next four years teaching combat survival. You serve?"

"Yeah."

"Navy SEALs, right?"

Street squirmed a little, realizing that Hondo probably knew a lot more than he was saying.

"That's what my file says," he agreed without commitment, and he hoped without expression.

"What did you do with them?"

"Besides rescue Marines who got lost?"

Hondo actually smiled a little. Street caught the change in his periphery. A little friendly fire.

"Sniper detail?" Hondo went on persistently. "Amphibious assaults? What?"

"My SEAL team commander always said that if anyone knew what I did, I'd failed."

Hondo paused. "Fair enough."

Street drew a sharp breath in through his nostrils, irritated by the questions. This was way-shit worse than cleaning guns. "You sure you don't want to sit in the back? Have me wear a little cap?"

"I like the view from the front," Hondo said. "But the cap's a nice idea."

Eased a little by the sass, Street mimed putting on a cap, then said, "So where're we going, Hondo?"

"Let's see what the weather's like in South Central."

And he picked up one of the folders on his lap.

Screaming pierced the Lincoln Heights neighborhood, interspersed with cursing in Spanish. It wasn't the kind of screaming that comes from fear, but from anger. And when some women got angry, could they scream.

This one could howl like a mad she-elephant.

"You get out of here right now!"

Officer Deacon Kaye tried to think of this overdone woman as just another civilian, but there was something really irritating about her.

"Just tell us where your boyfriend is!" he demanded as he and his partner rooted through the nasty little house, driven by the warrant they held and the fact that they'd been on this guy's trail for two weeks. By now they could just about smell him.

Literally. The air was sweet with the stink of those cigars he liked. They were close, really close!

Bam!

"Back door!" Deke shouted, and broke running through the house as if he knew where he was going.

His partner lunged for the woman—that was the last bit of movement he saw—just as she swung a frying pan. Before he heard the clang, he was out of the house and burning through the backyard, scattering chickens in every direction. Another version of screaming.

One yard ahead of him was a wiry homeboy in a warm-up suit, racing like wind through the cluttered backyards and alleys. As Deke ran ferociously after his target, he spoke into his radio's microphone.

"R-61-15 in foot pursuit! Heading south in the alley west of Defiance. One male black in Lakers purple!"

His voice traveled over the police airwaves in a hundred directions, seeking backup of whoever was in the right location to head off this punk, not to mention all the lazy twerp would-be militiamen out there who got their jollies by listening to real policemen at work on their scanner. It worked.

The radio transmission buzzed over the lines, through the air, into the city, and went right where it needed to go—to the Crown Victoria with the police radio specially mounted, specially authorized for undercover operations, deeply coveted right now by a certain highly trained and underused police career man. And the surly sergeant literally, if not spiritually, at his side.

"That's our guy talking!" Hondo blurted, worked up. "Where's he at?"

Street didn't bother to explain. He slammed on the brakes, throwing himself and Hondo forward—thank God for seat belts—and threw the car into reverse. The car threw up a couple of times as he gunned it backward for an entire block at the highest speed he could manage without losing control—not that he didn't come close.

"What the hell you doing, Navy SEAL!" Hondo choked.

Just then a joker in a jogging suit blew over a fence and sprinted directly toward them!

Followed—holy shit—by a big black cop on foot. Maybe on jets.

Street played a game of chicken with the runner, but the escapee took him up on it and sprinted right up over the hood of the car and the roof and the trunk—then the cop did the same. *Clatter clat clunk.*

"My car!" Hondo wailed.

The car slammed to a halt, and Street bolted out of the driver's seat. With the door open, the noises from outside flooded Hondo. Dogs barking, feet drumming, some woman shrieking in a Hispanic rage—

He smiled as he watched Street bullet after the cop and the purple streak. Pretty good . . .

Jim Street ran like a bird dog in hot pursuit. Everything he had been training himself to do over the past six months, enhancements of his SEAL training, maintenance of the body he was blessed with, and the quickness of eye and muscle he had at his command, came into play with a ferocity that surprised even him. He hadn't pursued a suspect in six months. He *wanted* this creep.

Maybe he wanted him almost as much as the cop who was beating him. Was this cop a SEAL too?

Naw . . . Street would know.

Within seconds he and the cop were dogging it shoulder to shoulder, and Street was beginning to pull ahead, but he got the idea it was only because he hadn't been chasing as long as the uniform. That was his only edge, he knew, so he kept his pride in his pocket for a change.

Their pounding feet ate up the alley in seconds, and some poor parked car got two big dents in its hood when they went over it. They dropped on the other side and bolted, soon pounding side by side through the complex alley system, barely keeping an eye on the suspect. They'd never had caught him on the straightaway, but the alleys dumped into backyards of some kind of apartment complex that confused the suspect into a couple of bad turns and for several seconds tied up the pursuit.

The confusion put Street and the big cop a little ahead now. The cop was obviously a good sprinter, but was losing his breath. Street sensed the advantage of a man who runs every single morning without fail.

"Take right!" the cop shouted. "I'm breaking left!"

Great! Permission from the officer to participate. That was all Street needed. He drew two quick breaths to max out his lungs and put all his concentration on his thighs and calves.

Power—he needed speed, not endurance. He had to let go.

Once his legs understood, he pulled ahead. The cop broke left like he said he would, and Street broke right. He compressed his body, stretched his legs, and bore down, concentrating on every stride, telescoping what was in front of him so he could sideswipe every Dumpster and jump every bit of trash without breaking his pace or even changing the flow of air over his body.

They chased the suspect through an auto shop, with a clang and ring of scattering tools and some pretty shocked looks from the men working inside and one lady waiting for her car.

The suspect almost knocked the lady down on his way through the office. That was when the cop and Street broke company and split around two different angles, working to cut the guy off, almost as if they'd worked together for years. They just both saw the opportunity and moved on it. Not bad. The move made Street feel like part of something he'd been missing out on.

And he knew it was working. The runner was starting to do crazy things, trying to go straight when there was nowhere to go and having to change his direction at the last second. He knew they were on his tail and he was panicking. He was bumping into things and skidding and even tripped once. The distance began to close. Two blocks—one and a half—one—

This felt great!

Was that music? Didn't sound like a boom box— not one from this neighborhood, anyway . . .

A parade!

6

WAS IT SAINT PATRICK'S DAY, OR WHAT? STREET NEVER paid attention to those things.

He and the cop and the runner weaved like linebackers, darting through a marching band in the long line of performers that was coming down the Lincoln Heights street. To their credit, even the suspect's, they didn't knock over one musician. The music didn't even stop.

Just as the runner escaped the parade and embarked on a long, straight run down a side street, Street knew he had a real chance of losing this guy. A straightaway would only serve the suspect. He gathered his strength, sucked in three sustaining breaths, and prepared to run even faster—

Gagggh—Hondo stepped out of nowhere and clotheslined the runner right in the throat. The suspect went down, with his legs in the air, still pumping. Street heard the impact through the pounding of his own blood in his ears. By the time he checked his own speed and managed to pull up, though it was well past Hondo when he and the cop actually got control over their own momentum, Hondo had flipped the jerk over and cuffed him. Just like that.

As Street rounded and came back, a twelve-year-old kid watching nearby said, "Damn, that was some Oakland Raider Jack Tatum action there!"

Hondo glanced. "What do you know about Jack Tatum?"

The kid just shrugged.

"Man, what do you run?" the cop gasped, looking at Street. "An eight-second forty-four?"

Street cleared his throat and nodded. He had to cough a couple of times, but he knew he could've gone ten more blocks, which made him—well, pretty happy. This was the first real foot pursuit he'd engaged in since he'd begun training seriously, determined to impress himself if not everybody else.

So far, so good.

Hondo pulled the purple guy to his feet and dragged him over to where Street and the cop were suffering their exhaustion.

"Officer Deacon Kaye?" Hondo began.

"Yeah, so?"

"Name's Hondo."

"I don't give a shit what your name is," the handsome black cop said. "Homeboy's my collar. Been after his ass for a month." He forcibly took possession of the suspect.

While Hondo smiled, a black lady on a nearby

porch wasn't so happy with what she saw, and snapped, "Don't you got nothin' better to do than haul another black man to jail? Just perpetuatin' the cycle, ain't ya?"

Street grimaced. *Wonder what talk show taught her that?*

The black cop had no apologies. He skewered the woman with a firm glare and said, "Let's see how liberal you are when he's breaking into your place and kicking your ass, lady."

He dragged his collar down the sidewalk, so sharply that both Street and Hondo had to hustle to catch up.

"You got a shit-load of collars in a nasty precinct," Hondo said to Kaye.

"I got the *most*," Kaye corrected. "I don't like it when they get away, so I don't let them."

"We noticed," Street agreed. "What'd he do anyway? We just heard about the foot pursuit, and we were only—"

"He's been mugging street vendors like they were little bird feeders and he's a squirrel."

"Street vending's not legal in this zone," Hondo commented, somewhat drably.

"Neither is mugging." A clear-cut passion showed in Kaye's eyes as he mopped sweat from his face. He took the crime personally.

Street knew that look, that passion. It wasn't always good. He knew it from inside, but also from the poison that had eaten Brian Gamble until he finally broke.

Still, the best cops are the ones who really believe they're out there protecting their very own mothers and sisters and kids, and they see their families in the face of every victim.

"There's an opening on my team in S.W.A.T.," Hondo said abruptly. "If you don't mind long hours, hard work, and getting dirty for low pay—"

The cop suddenly swung around, his black eyes all lit up. Street had learned from Kaye's folder Hondo brought with them. He was almost unknown just because he didn't make a big deal of his abilities, but his record was exemplary, and something about it had impressed Hondo. All this time Street had been killing himself to impress somebody, but this guy did it just by doing his job. How did things like this work, anyway? Maybe it was because he was black.

Maybe not.

"No, sir!" Kaye bolted. "I don't mind those things at all!"

He stuck out his hand for Hondo's, never even glancing at Street.

"Pack your bags, son," Hondo said. "You're going to S.W.A.T. school!"

"Where do you want me to report?" Kaye asked, controlling his tone, but not really hiding his enthusiasm. "And when? I can come right after I get dismissed today. Three hours, seventeen minutes!"

Hondo shrugged. "When you get off duty, come on over to the Academy at Elysian Park and find me. We've got to get to know each other if we're gonna put our lives on the line together."

"I won't let you down! See you guys later."

He strode off with his suspect. If he'd waited a couple of minutes, he could get a ride in a black-and-white, but Street got the idea Deacon Kaye wasn't the type to wait around.

"Where're you going?" Street asked.

Glowing with satisfaction, Kaye tossed a look over his shoulder. "I'm gonna arrest the street vendors. What else?"

The Crown Vic was rolling again. Now Street was sweaty and felt dirty. Hadn't even gotten a thank-you from the cop. Or a good-job from Hondo.

Nothing.

Just dirt.

The L.A. streets were busy now. It was midday and the roads were crowding up. Street clamped his lips and gritted his teeth to keep from speaking his mind. Beside him, Hondo thumbed through another folder. A very effective method of torture, this.

He was still throbbing from the adrenaline rush. It wasn't helping him drive, exactly, though.

"David Burress," Hondo read aloud. "Southwest Division. You know him?"

"No, I don't know him, Sergeant."

"Hondo."

"Right."

"Just drive."

Ten minutes later they stopped in front of a hot-dog pushcart, and in front of the cart was Uniformed Officer David Burress, peeled straight off the cover of the latest *Soap Opera Digest*. Even to guys, this guy looked . . . like Mount Olympus's idea of a guy. All the more irritating because of his Dudley DoRight attitude.

Street lagged back a couple of steps, not wanting any of that perfection to rub off, while Hondo talked to what's-his-wonderful.

"Your test scores are off the charts," Hondo was saying, of course, while he looked at the folder he had probably already memorized. "All the right references . . ."

"Thank you, Sergeant," Burress said, white teeth flashing.

"Hot dog with everything," Hondo interrupted himself. "And a Coke."

The hot-dog guy was on his best behavior. Hondo turned to Street, who simply said, "Same," without wanting to use his voice any more than necessary. It wasn't radio-ready, so what use was it?

Hondo motioned Burress toward the cart, but Prince Charming said, "Soy dog, please. Plain, on a wheat bun. And a tomato juice, if you've got it." Then he smiled at Hondo. "I'm a vegetarian."

And he reads to blind children every Saturday, Street grumbled inside, *between soup kitchens*.

As the hot-dog vendor assembled their order,

Hondo continued plumbing the personnel folder. "I'm confused by your file. You've been a cop for six years and never had a civilian complaint against you."

Officer Burress nodded and somehow did it with modesty. "I try to be courteous and professional with everyone I encounter."

Hondo hesitated. "The thing about S.W.A.T., Dave—"

"David."

"Right . . . David . . . the thing about S.W.A.T. is sometimes you got to get a little dirty behind a street collar. You know what I'm saying?"

There was another pause. Street just waited, watching.

"No," Burress finally admitted. And he had actually bothered to think about it, just to be considerate.

That was about the depth of the conversation. They wrapped it up, made polite—too polite—hums and hems and byes, then Hondo and Street collected their cardiobombs and got back into the Crown Victoria.

"Can't trust a man I can't have a steak with," Hondo commented briefly.

"Can't blame you," Street said, noting that they finally had something they could agree about. "Where next?"

"Somebody named Chris Sanchez. Get on the radio and track him down like a quail. I need me a real tough hombre, amigo."

They tracked, and it took some doing. Sanchez seemed to be in twelve places at once. After an hour and a half of hunting around Hollenbeck Station, forty-six blocks of patrol area, three bars, and two malls, Street followed Hondo through the halls of the emergency room of a small Santa Monica hospital, the name of which they'd forgotten by the time they got inside. The gun-and-knife show had already started.

All around them were the night's first wave of cases. Gunshot wounds, slashings, accidents, ODs, self-inflicteds, domestic quarrels. Treatment Room 4, the last intern had suggested.

Between rooms 3 and 4, they were halted by a struggle. A knot of uniformed officers was holding down a massive Hispanic with gang tattoos, pressing him to a gurney while a frustrated nurse chased a vein to start an IV on the guy.

Street shook his head in disgust. Chase 'em down, drag 'em in, give 'em taxpayer-funded emergency treatment, free medication, free legal representation, free religious counseling, free drug rehab, free media coverage to tell their tales, and they still spit in your eye and call you an oppressor.

Punks. Just hadn't been raised right.

He flashed mentally on the animals in the bank who had ruined his career because he was determined not to let them have one drop of blood that wasn't their own blood, men to whom the cops had been little more than the day's challenge in a lifetime of fights.

It was always somebody else's fault. They were all so sad and hopeless, held back and held down, never mind twelve years of free education and a million other offerings handed to them on silver platters by American society, paid for by somebody else's sweat.

Seemed the more they got for free, the less they appreciated what they had. No wonder some cops turned bitter, even turned bad. After this trouble-maker got faded into the penal system, ten more would rise to take his place, and the same scene would play itself out in city ERs all over the country.

"I'm looking for an injured officer," Hondo blurted to the first nurse he could corral. "Name's Sanchez. Chris Sanchez."

Street could see in Hondo's face the hope that Sanchez wasn't hurt so badly that his chances at the new S.W.A.T. team could be diminished. Hondo wanted the team on line almost immediately, if Street read the signs right.

Who cares? I'm just the driver. What do I care if all their legs are broken at once?

The nurse pointed to a curtained area. "On the other side of that curtain. Getting sewn up."

"Who's the guy on the gurney?" Street asked, pointing to a huge Mexican with a whole lot of bruises and scratches, and a pair of cuffs keeping him in place.

"He's the one your officer brought in," the nurse said, and she left them to think about it.

"Reminds me of my third divorce," Hondo commented.

Street blinked. "She got violent with you?"

"Yeah. With my wallet."

They walked up to the Mexican, and Street tried not to grin as he said, "Bad day, huh?"

"Kiss my ass, *esse*," the creep mentioned pleasantly. He was really not pleased to deal with another cop.

Hondo laughed. "I already like this guy! Four years in Metro, passed the S.W.A.T. qualifications three times. Fuller always rejected him."

He handed Sanchez's file to Street for some reason. Why?

Street accommodated him by looking. "Maybe there's a reason. Got a few red marks."

Hondo glanced at him. Did that mean Sanchez could beat somebody up, or that he *liked* beating somebody up? Sometimes there was a thin partition between what made a cop and what made a criminal, at least in the soul.

He knew that in person. Some cops would make great criminals, and some criminals would make great cops. Street thought about how fine a thread ran between these two eternally linked worlds, and he had to repress a shudder of foreboding.

He followed Hondo over to the curtained examining area. Street didn't wait to be invited, but just pulled back the curtain.

There was a woman behind it, sitting on a gurney in her bra and trousers, as a doctor stitched up a laceration.

"Sorry," Hondo said. "Wrong room."

"Who you looking for?" the woman asked.

"Chris Sanchez."

"I'm Sanchez. Listen, if you're Internal Affairs, that guy came after me with double-edged razor blades in his mouth. I had to put him down hard. I'm sick of dealing with these bullshit complaints just because some *vato* doesn't like getting thrown to the pavement by a woman."

Hondo laughed. "I look like IAD to you?"

"Not really," she agreed, but tentatively. "Who are you?"

"That guy back there had a hundred pounds on you."

"So? Just takes a couple of extra punches."

Street glowered in both respect and suspicion. Extra punches, a supreme knowledge of leverage and balance, maybe some Judo, yoga, and about a year's worth of steady practice. She was being really, really modest. Just like a woman?

Or like an officer who believed in herself and knew what she could do? Sounded familiar.

He started to turn to leave, but Hondo's next question completely floored him.

"Want to work for S.W.A.T.?" Hondo asked bluntly.

Street flinched, almost for a minute thinking Hondo was speaking to him. But he wasn't—he was speaking to . . . oh, God . . . Chris*tine* Sanchez!

"No," Sanchez said in a small gasp. "Just enjoy applying all the time!"

*   *   *

"Gas it up and return it."

Street peered unhelpfully at Hondo, feeling the stiffness of a day in the car when he really wanted to be somewhere else. He didn't think there was anything that would make him want to be back in the gun cage, but guess what. They stood outside the Crown Vic, which had become his new prison. Not only did he have to drive this fart around town, but he had to drive him to interview prospective members of the new team. Talk about driving nails into Street's coffin and twisting them.

"Am I looking at another day of chauffeur duty?" he asked bluntly, not hiding his disgruntlement at the idea.

"Team's almost filled." Hondo cocked a hip at the concept, both satisfied and shielded.

"Not that it hasn't been fun," Street said, and barely managed not to spit.

Hondo shrugged and started to walk away, but then he turned back to Street and said, "I still got one more spot. You think of anyone I'm overlooking?"

Street's shoulders hurt from the runaround. This guy was in Fuller's pocket, or somebody's, somebody who hated Jim Street.

"This a game?" he asked. "Or a test?"

"Little bit of both."

"I'm a little old for games." Street drably turned back toward his favorite waste of time, the Crown Vic. How many of his fellow officers had seen him driving Mr. Daisy around?

"Fine. How'd you like to be back on S.W.A.T?"

Street paused, silent. He honestly didn't know what to think or do. Was this another way of tormenting him?

Was it a real question or a challenge or what? Or a joke?

"Don't try telling me," Hondo went on, "you're not dying for another chance."

The pit of Street's stomach got real hard.

"It's not gonna happen," he said.

"Then what they hell are you doing hanging around the cage?"

"It's a job."

"And S.W.A.T.'s a-calling. Five minutes with you, I can tell you still got the bug. All you got to do is say yes."

Street turned to him, doing everything he could to contain himself, both joy and anger.

"It's not up to me or you," he said, almost gagging. "I got a history here."

"Well, good," Hondo responded. "Let's talk about that. I heard the rumors about you, your old partner . . . you give him up in that room?"

"No." Street's voice suddenly hurt.

" 'Cause a team's got to trust each other."

Street's glare turned hard. "I'm not on your team."

Hondo considered him for a blank second or two.

"You've been sitting in that cage for six months, waiting for a second chance," he said finally. "I'm getting one. I'd like to give you one too."

Suddenly the whole garage seemed completely empty except for the two of them. Their voices carried a slight echo, like something out of a dream.

"Fuller'll never sign off on it."

"Let me handle that paper-pushing prick." Hondo moved a little closer. Just enough to more or less cement the moment. And what a moment for them both! "You want on my team," he added, "be at roll call at seven sharp."

Street held his mental ground. "Not interested."

Hondo turned, and this time he really did leave. He walked out of the Metro garage, his booted feet clicking some on the pavement, and his absence creating a kind of vacuum.

Street stood there alone. He'd pleaded, hoped, mourned, fought for this moment. Now that it was here, he actually wasn't sure what to do. If he showed up at seven o'clock in the morning, he could just as easily be shot down in front of all the other officers chosen for this team.

Hondo hadn't believed him when he said he wasn't interested. Somehow Street knew that. He knew when somebody was making a double-or-nothing bet on him.

Would that be the moment when he would find out that even Sergeant Hondo Harrelson couldn't jump over the unhappy force of Captain Fuller? Did he want to go through this again?

If he didn't, why had he hung around in the cage? Hondo had a point.

Right now, he just wasn't sure.

And the strangest wish came over him. He wanted, more than anything, to go out into the mists of the world and ask Brian Gamble what to do.

The French Bistro was closing up for the night, but only to the public.

The Lincoln Town Car pulled up outside while all the other cars were pulling away, some to go home, others to look for other bars that were open later.

Alex Lupin and G.Q. got out almost simultaneously, as if choreographed. G.Q. quietly opened the Bistro door for Lupin.

The place appeared empty.

Lupin simply said, "We leave in an hour."

Inside was a private party in full progress. Certain people had been allowed to stay past closing time. Unknowns had been escorted out. Two guards stood at the insides of the doors, scanning the crowd constantly. There were gorgeous girls everywhere, and bottles of Cristal adorning the occasion. The two guards almost stopped Lupin as he entered, obscured by swirls of cigar and cigarette smoke, but then they realized who he was and let him pass.

There were surprised reactions all over, of varying types, and he made nice by waving and smiling here and there. They were happy to see him.

Then his uncle saw him and thundered toward

him through the parting crowd, waving his arms for a big body hug, something fairly cocky for a life-time thug like Martin Gascoigne.

"Alex!" Martin bellowed. "When did you get here?!"

"Happy birthday, Uncle. Surprise," Lupin said cheerily, unintimidated by the big, big man.

As he relaxed a little, someone pushed a glass of champagne into his hand.

He looked at the bubbling liquid and realized that he could very fairly drink to himself tonight, and not to his uncle, birthday or no birthday.

This was going to be a good night, the start of something new, strong, and terrible. When the night was over, he would be in charge of every-thing he could reach.

His reach was long.

7

CAPTAIN FULLER LEANED BACK IN HIS CHAIR. HE SCANNED folders of Hondo's chosen few with a practiced dispassion. Hondo sat in another chair at the far end of the office, not letting Fuller see that it was bothering him to wait so long. Fuller was doing this deliberately, stalling, pretending to frown over the files. The two of them had a history too. Street wasn't the only cop in Los Angeles with a rocky record. Hondo liked his rocks.

Eventually Fuller had to speak up, say something, almost anything to forward the moment. After all, they couldn't sit here till tomorrow just because he was playing a game, could they? Even captains had to eat.

Fuller lolled in his chair and pressed his lips in fake thought.

"If Dallas P.D. wanted you so bad," he said slowly, "you should've taken the job there."

"I got a thing for palm trees." Hondo had his answer ready to go. Knew that would come up.

Fuller put down the file he was looking at and picked up the next one. All it took was one glance.

"Is this a joke?"

"I never joke with you, Tom."

"There's a reason there's never been a woman on S.W.A.T."

"Same reason there were never any black men in S.W.A.T. till I started?"

Ah, the race card. Sometimes it could be just perfect. Hondo knew the real reason—same reason a lot of people were nervous about putting women on the front lines in the military. He knew it wasn't exactly the same as the difference between two men who were different colors. There were just certain hardwired problems when women were involved. Men and women really were different. Men tended to protect women, even when the women didn't need protecting. That caused distraction and loss of concentration. Could happen.

Could a lady the size of Sanchez carry a two-hundred-pound partner out of a dangerous situation, say a fire or an accident? That had nothing to do with skill, but the simple logistics of upper-body strength. She might be able to outshoot every expert around, but she would probably have to actually shoot somebody to prove it. There were jocks out there in the mean streets who just wouldn't take a woman cop seriously until she was finally forced to prove herself the hard way.

Sanchez wasn't exactly six feet tall and two-ten with a silhouette like a bull buffalo. Hard to imagine a bunch of drunken bikers standing down in front of her, badge or not. She'd have to kill somebody. It wasn't like there weren't legitimate arguments.

He held his breath. Breaking ground wasn't his favorite thing, whatever his reputation said.

"No," Fuller said, "not the same reason."

"Well, Tom, I think she can do the job," Hondo said simply, hoping not to get into the longer conversation, which he knew he'd probably lose.

Fuller looked up. "We're not partners anymore, Dan. I outrank you. I've earned my title. Please use it."

He was right. Only fair.

"Sorry, Captain."

Fuller's attitude mellowed somewhat. "The Chief's making me take you back. He's tired of losing his best officers to other cities."

Hondo couldn't help a flutter of surprised pride. "He thinks I'm one of his best officers?"

"But he's giving me full oversight. And trust me—you got no room for error. You can have T.J. and Boxer and this new guy, Deacon Kaye. I'm going to have to pass on the other two, though. Sanchez is a woman, and Street's on my shit list."

"I'm on your shit list. I'm on the team."

"You work for me now, and it's my team to choose."

Hondo bristled, but contained himself. "With all due respect, Captain, other leaders get to pick their teams."

"So can you. Just pick two new people."

"All I want," Hondo pressed, leaning forward some, "is for you to give me the team I want. Even let you call it 'The Shit List Team.' That way, anything goes wrong, you can put all the blame on me. Just like the old days."

Ouch. Incoming Stinger.

Fuller knew he was getting played, but he also knew he held all the cards. He paused, put the files down on his desk, folded his fingers, and leaned forward on his desk.

"Okay," he said. "You got your team. But when you fail, this Sanchez woman's back in Traffic Control or wherever she came from, and you and your boy Street are plain gone. Not just S.W.A.T. The Force. You understand what I'm saying?"

It was quite a speech. Part of it surprised Hondo and part sure didn't. They were both making big bets, the kind of bets that made national news when losses were counted.

L.A. was already in the news the hard way. If they made this high-profile attempt and it turned sour, this would make the city a media laughingstock.

So what would be different?

Oh, what the hell. He'd won for now.

Understand?

He stood up and headed for the door.

"Always have, Tom," he said.

Almost everyone was gone. The big private birthday party had wound down slowly and steadily, with most of the guests staying long enough to endear themselves to Alex Lupin and his big Uncle Martin. Some of them didn't even know why they needed to ingratiate themselves to either of these men, but power had a certain aroma and everyone here had caught a whiff. They knew where their futures could be and wanted to plant seeds. Especially the girls. What an easy night this had been.

Only Lupin, Martin, and a circle of six associates were left, nursing the last of their wine. Lupin checked his watch, but didn't really register what it said.

"I'm leaving now," he said.

"No, Alex!" Martin crowed. "We have wine and cognac from home! Please!"

"I really must go. I have duties. I'm running the business now."

Uncle Martin only laughed and patted Lupin's cheek. This made Lupin fume inwardly.

"Yes, you keep very busy," Martin said. "But never forget . . . your father runs the business."

"No, Uncle Martin. I retired him."

Martin's smile dissolved. Perhaps, he was realizing, this wasn't a joke.

Lupin felt a dark flash rise in his own eyes.

Martin suddenly laughed again. "Come on! Look at you. Always so serious. He told me no such thing!"

He took a swig of his wine.

Snick.

The knife was in Lupin's hand now, blade open. "Because he can't speak. I slit his throat."

Martin Gascoigne had a chance to realize what the truth was, to see reality, but no chance to react. Alex Lupin simply leaned forward and with a practiced motion ran the knife across his uncle's carotid artery, laying it open, then continued the motion across the underside of his uncle's fleshy throat.

When he withdrew the knife, the entire side and front of Martin's throat spurted blood from a gash that would fascinate even Madame Tussaud. All the hours practicing on animals had allowed for a perfect, calm motion of slaughter. No violence, no struggle. Perfect.

Around him, his uncle's associates were stony with terror. They said nothing, didn't move, didn't dare.

Lupin stood up and raised the knife, gazing down at his uncle's shuddering form. Not quite dead yet. That would come in a few minutes. The gurgle would eventually stop.

"I won't tolerate people's stealing from me," he said. "Understood?"

A few seconds lumbered past until the associates realized he was talking to them, rather than making some kind of post-assassination poetry.

They remained quiet as G.Q. handed Lupin a tablecloth which he used to wipe the knife. There wasn't much blood, though. Not on the knife, at least. He liked to be clean.

He stepped back, to keep his shoes out of the spurts and puddling.

"Drop him in the ocean," he said.

G.Q. nodded.

Lupin closed the knife and tossed it to G.Q. "Mail this to me."

No one knew what that was all about, not even G.Q. Lupin thought about the considerate dopey customs agents and how easy it was to pretend to be good.

Interesting—the innocent people had trouble pretending to be bad, but he could easily fool all the fools out there by pretending to be innocent. That element of human nature always served him, the idea that most people wanted to believe others were decent. Benefit of the doubt always played in his favor.

It helped that he was physically not very threatening. He was the man next door, the one everyone thought was sweet and kind and wouldn't step on an ant.

They were right.

He just made sure all the ants were working for him and all the queens bowed to him. This one night would play in his favor for years. He wouldn't have to kill anyone else personally for a long time. Not until he needed to make another point.

He left the Bistro and took his victory tour in Uncle Martin's Mercedes. G.Q. would take care of the Town Car, but right now Lupin felt like cruising alone, enjoying his new superiority on his own, on the great Sunset Boulevard.

He had always liked Sunset. Here were all the latest and greatest clubs and hotels, a glistening strip, world-famous for good reason, a sparkling place to be when one felt grand. He drove slowly, enjoying himself, flirting with girls in other cars and chatting with transvestites who were stuck in traffic. He enjoyed watching unusual people and thinking about ways to control them along with all the usual, predictable people. He liked a challenge.

By the time he noticed that he was being tailed by two motorcycle policemen, the sirens were already going off and the lights were flashing in his rearview mirror. What was this all about? Hadn't Uncle Martin kept up the license?

The cop was a woman. He could take care of this easily, but decided to play it out. Perhaps she was simply bored.

He decided not to take action. She had a partner back there. Two cops was different from just one woman.

"Hello," Lupin said, putting up the fake accent. "Good evening!"

The lady cop stood slightly back from the driver's window. "Sir," she greeted, "may I see your license, registration, and proof of insurance?"

"I am visit United States," Lupin said. "I have passport."

"Let me see it. Whose car is this?"

"This car? Yes, the six hundred. Very nice car." He fished through the glove box for the papers. "Belong to my uncle."

"Your uncle's car? Okay." She took the papers. "Thank you. Please wait."

She crossed back to her gleaming Harley, parked in the glow of a bright street lamp. After a moment she came back, with her partner. "Is your uncle Martin Gascoigne?" she asked.

"Yes, Uncle Martin. See, we are okay!" He smiled.

"Sorry," she said, "but there's an arrest warrant in that name, and I have to detain you and this vehicle until I can verify who you are."

He let his smile go away and widened his eyes in doll-like perplexity. "I don't understand. . . ."

"Please step out of the car."

By the time his feet hit the pavement, he had already realized he couldn't fool her.

He would have to make a new plan.

LOS ANGELES COUNTY JAIL

His attorney's name was Kathy. She was cute, confident, very young, malleable, and had the right connections through her family, who had been working for Martin Gascoigne for years. It had long been forgotten who was doing whom the most good.

Alex Lupin was under arrest, but still in street clothes. He hadn't quite been booked yet, though there was quite a bit of whispering going on. And glances.

He took the seat across the bare little table from her, giving nothing away in his expressions.

"It's great to finally meet you," she said in a perky way that came off as annoying.

"How much longer?" he asked.

"Not long. It's all very standard."

"I know. But I have a flight to catch."

She looked disappointed. "You pay me a lot of money. Let me earn it."

She had cut to the chase. He liked that. He did pay her a lot. He would continue, he decided now, to do so. There was something about her that made him willing to wait. He wanted more than just to get out. He wanted his record completely wiped clean. Gone.

So she would earn her money today for sure. His future certainly did not aim toward a cell and a shared toilet.

LOS ANGELES POLICE DEPARTMENT TRAINING GROUNDS

Street got there before the sun had even crested the low-lying palms. That meant he had to stand and wait by the locked door for Hondo or somebody else with a key to show up. He tried to act as if he always stood around doorways, but certainly not because he was overanxious or anything.

"You're here awful early." Hondo strode up, looking at his watch.

Street turned. "Traffic was lighter than usual."

"The roads must've been damn near empty," Hondo countered, unlocking the door as he managed, with effort, not to smile. "Come on in, then."

They stepped inside, and that's when Street caught the smile in his periphery. Busted.

Oh, well. So he was excited. That was better than other things, right?

Hondo's tone was that of a man protesting too much. Street got the idea that he had by no means a lock on this assignment. One screw-up or a whiff of attitude and he would be back in his little cage for good. Street was clam-happy and enjoying delusions of almost everything. He had to bite his lip to keep down a very unmacho giggle. He felt nervous, but in a terrific way. He was back after six long months, jumping ahead of dozens of other candidates who were younger and had cleaner records, and what the hell, when your mother's being held hostage, do you really want some kid with a spotless record going in after her?

A spotless record means nothing's happened to you worth spotting up.

Yeah, that's it, Jimmy, that's the truth you're telling yourself. Keep talking.

A few minutes, very few, later, Deke and Boxer rolled in, also early, then T.J. They were all aware of one another, but not really talking. Street got the feeling they thought they were the old pros and he was the rookie. He was particularly aware of Boxer, but tried not to single him out.

Too late. Here he came.

"What'd you do to my sister?" he asked.

Street fiddled with his duffel bag, then finally decided that wouldn't work on this particular subject, and turned to face Boxer like a man.

"Nothing."

T.J. came along to help, but not Street. "Not what I heard," he interjected.

Suddenly the room was a couple of degrees warmer. Not in a nice way, either.

No getting around this.

Boxer persisted, "My mom says she's real broken up over you."

"Don't know why," Street said honestly. "She left me, not the other way around."

T.J. had the nerve to say, "A case of the clap'll do that to a girl."

Over there, Deke was pointedly staying out of the testosterone-fest, but was driven to mutter, "Something about this team I should know?"

Boxer gave Street a bitter glare. "What they hell did you do to make my little sister leave?"

Street met the glower firmly. "She's twenty-eight. And trust me, she's not so little."

Boxer lunged for him. Street was ready—had seen the anger rise in Boxer's eyes—and knew that nobody really liked to hear that his sister had grown up into something another man could appreciate in those kinds of ways. Street struggled, but not very passionately.

All he needed was more enemies.

Maybe if he let Boxer throw him around a little, Boxer would feel like he'd won something, or at least brought some honor to his sister. This was a fight between two young men with attitudes, who had once thought they might be brothers-in-law. How hard could they really go after each other? Which one dared actually do damage so the relationship could never go back? Some things weren't elastic.

Not hard enough to both the other men, who just watched and made silent bets in their heads. T.J. loved what he saw, the shithead.

Deke, though, finally interrupted before anything got out of hand. He got between them just before the moment exploded into something a hell of a lot uglier. Just when Street thought he might not get out of this day without some serious tooth breaking, the lady cop Christine Sanchez came in the door, dressed in full S.W.A.T. gear.

Hondo and Street were the only ones whose jaws didn't hit the floor.

"Who are you?!" T.J. broke.

Sanchez came into the room all the way, her eyes hard and her lips soft, posture just right in the uniform, and completely comfortable in the body armor.

"Who the hell are you?" she tossed back, controlling her tone. She clearly understood and had expected the reaction. She let them know with her attitude that they were on probation regarding her presence here. The first women on every new team in the world had always had to endure and tolerate these moments. The first lady doctor, the first lady soldier, pirate, astronaut, governor, mayor, from

Amelia Earhart to Condoleezza Rice. Sanchez was really just the latest in a long honorable line.

She seemed to know that.

Street leaned to T.J. and said, "Guess you're not the prettiest one here anymore."

T.J. shot him an acid look.

Were they really this backward? Street knew plenty of female cops. They all did. It wasn't that. Still, a five-foot-four female cop is going to be forced to protect herself. And then there was the simple man-thing about protecting women. Street knew he had it. It was natural. How could he fight that and let Sanchez take a bullet instead of some innocent victim? Could he do it? The idea of choosing made him nervous. Men didn't like to let women get hurt.

What was wrong with that, exactly?

Sanchez had looked Hondo right in the eye and insisted she could do this job. She demanded it based on her record. She deserved it. S.W.A.T. needed people like that—pushy, driven, secure in themselves, and willing to run into a hail of bullets and not away from it. Every man—person—on S.W.A.T., Street included, had possessed the self-confidence and moxie to beat down any social pretense of humility and just flat-out scream, "I want the fucking job!"

Sanchez was screaming that now, just with her eyes.

Street couldn't help a little smile of approval right through his haze of testosterone.

Hondo interrupted them just before things turned into a commercial for a reality TV show. He came in wearing full S.W.A.T. fatigues, the sight of which put them into a whole other mode.

"I see you've all become acquainted," he said. "Let's get going."

Would it be best to explain their personal history to Hondo? Tell him that T.J. couldn't stand Street and Street was real tired of Boxer and the girlfriend thing and all?

And that Boxer was pissed and wanted an excuse to defend his sister?

That none of them was crazy about putting their lives into the hands of a woman backup who couldn't possibly drag them out of a situation because the physics just weren't on her side?

Naw . . . better keep all that to himself for now. Street wanted to at least spend one full day on the S.W.A.T. team before they threw him off for good.

They went into the classroom, but nobody got comfortable. There was no point. This wasn't a bookwork sort of training session. Hondo had something to say, and after that they would be going into the hardest physical struggle any of them had experienced since the military.

"This is simple," Hondo said, also wanting to get the ball rolling. "L.A.P.D. S.W.A.T. is the most honored, most respected, and most professional police division in the world. The instant you do not treat it as such, you are out. Of the ten thousand cops in

L.A.P.D., only sixty-seven are S.W.A.T. Sixty-six men and one woman."

Sanchez couldn't help a nervous and excited smile. Boxer and T.J. were annoyed, but said nothing. Street countered them, just to get their goats, by nodding in approval to Sanchez and letting her know she was welcomed at least by one of them.

Deke had gone real quiet. He seemed to have mixed feelings but wasn't making judgments yet.

Hondo waited until the silent communication faded.

Then he waited a little longer, until they were all looking at him and concentrating on him and not their own thoughts and lives. He slowly went on.

"S.W.A.T. is a lifesaving organization, not a life-taking one. That's why the FBI and Secret Service come here to train with us. We get the call to match up with the worst of the worst. You will be prepared for anyone and anything. Nine times out of ten, you'll never fire a weapon or find yourself in danger. It's the tenth time I'm training you for."

A quiet blanket of awareness dropped over the room. Something changed, very subtle. Their new commanding officer had just explained to them that whatever they were expecting would probably not be what they would face, that they couldn't possibly anticipate any event where they would be needed, that a whole other kind of quickness of mind would be needed when the special team was called to action.

They knew Hondo had a reputation, not always

good, not for going by the book all the time, and that was probably the reason he was here to do this, reactivated to bring the L.A.P.D. back to the top of its form, to put the force on edge and make it lean, and to let the public know by this team's actions and success that things had changed.

"Lose your focus, your fire, or your determination, and you or the person next to you will wind up dead. Trust me. I've seen it. You will do what I say, chapter and verse, until our final exam. Questions?"

For a few seconds no one said anything. Then Sanchez went ahead and raised her hand.

"What's the final?" she asked. "Multiple choice?"

Hondo paused.

"Multiple terrorist," he said.

8

ROPES IN THEIR HANDS. CHOPPER BLADES WHOPPING overhead. Ten pounds of gear, more of weapons, belts, harnesses, boots, protective Kevlar, kneepads, elbow pads. The warm Southern California air pumping down from the helicopter. Pulses hammering almost louder than the blades.

And down they swept from the great dragonfly in the sky, shushing their way through the pumping open air like spiders coming down thin lines of webbing. They landed roughly, but everyone stayed on foot, broke the cable connections, twirled their weapons into their hands, and ran like hell for the hotel entrance.

Hondo timed them, and wasn't happy.

Jim Street was behind Boxer as they blew toward the bungalows and went to the first one, which was their target. He knew Hondo was watching, knew the clock was ticking, and heard

114

his blood pound in his ears. He couldn't shake the idea that this was his one chance, his last chance, to get back where he wanted. He knew he was being given unusual dispensation, that his chance hung on a thread of good behavior.

Good behavior—he'd thought he was behaving perfectly right all those times with Brian. He'd made his best judgments every time, backed up his partner on the spear of the action, and come out alive, with all the right other people alive and the bad ones dead. Wasn't that pretty good behavior?

In these days of public relations police work, of eyes in the skies and dash cams, every couch potato and talking head was a backseat driver for the cops. Shouldn't this have happened? Shouldn't they have known? Shouldn't someone have anticipated? Why were those particular weapons out? Couldn't they have waited two more seconds?

And the airwaves were cluttered with would-be authors, private detectives, retired cops, and self-proclaimed experts on everything from surveillance to forensics, all prodded to critique what they hadn't witnessed and predict the unpredictable, and like idiots they all tried. How else could a dozen networks fill up twenty-four hours of news?

Anything done by any cop that might be slightly out of the ordinary would end up on TV eventually, being critiqued by zillions of amateurs.

Just try to get that out of your mind. You'd have to be in a coma to forget that and just do the job. Look what happened to Brian and me, and nobody even got that on camera. But we still made the news ten times over. Everybody was having a say about it except us.

Street shook out of his reverie just in time to rocket in front of Boxer, while Boxer ducked back into the agreed position. Street moved forward like a bullet and kicked in the bungalow door, then dodged aside to cover Deke and Sanchez as they swept inside.

Pop pop pop pop pop! Their weapons plastered the room, taking down two targets.

Too much ammo used for only two targets, Street noted, and logged the information away.

When the shooting ended, Hondo was right there.

"The entry was good," he said. "But if you like waking up the next day, better shoot those mothers on the move."

Street could tell that Deke and Sanchez were befuddled. Probably hadn't even realized they'd stopped running in order to open fire. Those things could happen. It would've been easy to snicker, and Street thought he might have heard one from T.J., but then admitted he probably didn't.

Keep control over those resentments, pal. You need these people.

The thought left a bad taste. He knew it was true, though, and fought to bury the spurs.

The second entry was simply the second bungalow. They wouldn't have the rush of the helicopter fast-roping, but that had gone smoothly and wouldn't be repeated, at least not today. By the time training was over, they all knew they'd have their lifetime fill of helicopters and rappelling and lines and harnesses and hard landings.

The second bungalow had also been stocked with cardboard bad guys, all set up by Hondo, arranged to confuse and surprise them, to be as un-predictable as possible, just like real people. This was supposed to be a covert entry, the kind the bad guys never heard or saw coming.

It meant a whole other kind of police work, a different breed of S.W.A.T. action—and it made Street think again of Gamble and that ill-fated entry that had saved the woman's life. He remembered his heart pounding and his lungs aching because he was trying not to breathe loudly. He remembered the sweat puddling under his arms and between his fingers and toes, the heat of the fatigues and the pressure of the body armor. He relived it all as he gave a hand signal to his teammates to don their gas masks.

Beside him, Sanchez had some trouble. Impatient, he turned and assisted her, securing the mask in place. She nodded her thanks, but he ignored her.

Boxer tapped his watch.

They began moving again—

And were stunned by the blast of a shotgun as the wall in front of them virtually exploded.

Hondo stood in the doorway, a shotgun smoking in his hands.

Oh, shit, they'd never even gotten inside. Beautiful, right?

"Sanchez, are you gonna clear that corner or what?" Hondo roared. "Remember, we're in the suspect's environment!"

"Yes, sir!" Sanchez instantly responded.

Street pressed back against the wall, deeply annoyed at this fuckup. He had to battle with himself to remember it was a lapse in judgment or timing or something and really had nothing to do with her being a woman, unless you could chalk it up to the plain fact that women tended to hesitate and take fewer chances than men. Sometimes that worked out. Sometimes not. Today . . . not.

"You better get in killing mode," Hondo warned.

Suddenly Sanchez ripped off her mask. "I am in killing mode," she said.

"Then why you smiling?" Hondo asked.

She actually laughed and shook the mask. "'Cause it tickles me!"

The tension dissolved. An instant later everybody was laughing.

Kind of took the steam out of the men.

They needed a few minutes to get back into the teeth-gritting mode, and when they did, Hondo broke the news that they would be doing the helicopter entry again right away.

Then they did it again.

By the end of the day they were exhausted. That's when he took them out on night maneuvers.

Message: There is no end to S.W.A.T.'s day.

By the next morning every one of them was

feeling the day before. Muscles ached, eyes were sore, fingers throbed, shoulders were tender. Even Jim Street, who had been unremitting with himself physically for the past six months, had to admit he just hurt all over.

Of course, he didn't admit it out loud.

Luckily, the next day was spent at the rifle range. A chance to train without drain. Street harbored a certain satisfaction that they weren't doing chopper entries and bungalow blasting today, because quite simply that meant their time had improved and Hondo was, at least temporarily, satisfied with the previous day's actions and results.

Now Hondo stood on the sidelines with the team sprawled out in sniper positions along the shooting-range firing line. Hondo had binoculars up to his eyes, and he was peering at the targets a hundred yards away.

"T.J.'s sitting on two pair, looking for the boat."

T.J. aimed and fired almost immediately.

Street could just barely make out the cards, fifty-two playing cards taped to the targets. T.J.'s shot ripped through the six of hearts.

"He got it," Hondo reported. "Sixes over fours. Street's next. Sitting on three aces."

Street put his weapon to his cheek and fired. Once, twice . . . three . . . four times.

"Four aces," Hondo said. "Very tough to beat. Deke? Let's see what you got."

Deke took aim more carefully than T.J. or Street, considered his target the way he might if he were actually sniping a suspect, and his bullet tore through the ten of spades, but fired only once.

"Spade flush. That's not gonna cut it."

Street leaned back and squinted into the sunshine. "Hondo, isn't that a straight flush?"

Hondo put the binoculars back up to his eyes and checked it out. The eight, nine, ten, jack, and queen . . . all spades.

"Deke-san!" he bellowed. "That's a damned straight flush!"

Deke smiled and slapped hands with Street. "Beats four aces in Compton any day of the week!"

"You slobs can shoot, I can't argue with that."

"Problem is keeping us from shooting each other," Street mumbled.

"Don't tempt me," Boxer snapped back.

Street looked at him. "*She* . . . left *me*."

Hondo groaned. "You guys are making me puke. *As the S.W.A.T. Team Turns.* Put it in your pockets and let's get back to the bungalows."

"Awww!" T.J. complained. "I thought—"

"I know what you thought," Hondo cut off. "You thought I was going to ease off on you. Well, you thought wrong, sisters! On your feet! Let's fly, fly, fly!"

Bungalow 3 was a sitting duck. The team was hyped, partly because they thought they were off the hook for the day and they were mad that this bungalow wasn't pizza with double cheese, and partly because they were just plain jazzed to be doing this.

Hondo led the way on this maneuver. They stacked up along an outside wall, then Hondo motioned to Deke, who came up with a steel ram and crashed the door off its hinges. The noise barked through the quiet evening, and the team launched their crisis entry. They burst inside and fanned out in perfect form, which made Jim Street realize for the first time that they were starting to read one another's posture, moves, body language, and timing. Instead of being several separate units with big talents, they were turning into a team. Hondo had been right to make them do this again, and right to give them a break from it at the firing range. The breather had galvanized something in their brains that now started clicking.

The real snap came in Street's mind when he almost tripped on an end table in the bungalow and who but Boxer himself elbowed him back to balance. The automatic move was a surprise, yet had been so natural and comforting that Street responded with a tap of gratitude on Boxer's arm.

Just that, nothing more, but what a change. And in only a day. Could they trust each other with their lives?

He still didn't know, though he was getting closer to making that bet.

"Outstanding," Hondo congratulated. "I'm starting to like you guys."

Imagine that!

Street ruminated on just how hard that had been to imagine just a day ago. Things had changed fast, possibly because of Hondo's unremitting drill-sergeant style, and otherwise because he had picked the right people. No matter the friction between them, the team had an electrical connection that had awakened quickly. Street had worked with others on the force and not felt this kind of mutual readability for months, and sometimes never. He'd even had partners he'd never clicked with, no matter how the TV shows insisted that disparate partners always eventually jelled. Didn't always happen.

In the locker room things changed. Street stayed off to the side, not quite at cozy with these people when there wasn't a weapon in his hands. Funny how the good feelings dissolved when he had to look them in the eyes. If only he could live, sleep, eat, and play while wearing full body armor. Maybe he'd be comfortable then.

But he couldn't. He had to come back to being just plain Jim Street, fellow officer and somebody who could actually just have lunch with the same people he had to work with. He hadn't picked this team. He would've picked different people. Oddly, the only one he felt at ease with so far was Sanchez. She didn't threaten him the way Boxer and T.J. did. Deke—didn't have any reaction to him at all. Except maybe that they were two completely different kinds of men, with different tracks of life.

"Aw, man, my wife's all worried about my being in S.W.A.T.," Deke was saying, as if reading Street's mind and nailing the reason for the gap between them right on its head.

"They always are at first," Boxer told him.

"She's like, how's she gonna take care of the kids if something happens to me, right? So I call State Farm, looking for some extra life insurance, and when I tell the sister I work S.W.A.T., guess what she does."

"Laughs?" T.J. suggested.

"Hangs up?" Boxer threw in.

"The woman laughs her ass off, then she hangs up on me!"

Street glanced at them. He wanted to speak up, but couldn't. He wanted to point out that anybody on the S.W.A.T. team was at more risk just driving to the danger scene than actually being there. Car accidents killed a hell of a lot more policemen than police work ever did, just like some folks were afraid of flying, but they were in a hell of a lot more rush driving to the airport than they ever would be on a plane. Same with being a police officer. By far, most of the work was cleanup. Rarely were cops ever actually on the scene of an incident while it happened. Most often they were called during or just after, and had to chase around to find anything worth talking about later.

Special Weapons and Tactics activity was a little more risky, but the training and procedure eliminated a huge degree of the actual danger. Civilians just didn't understand.

Life insurance workers, though, should know

better. Statistics weren't that hard to track down. Street had never had trouble getting life insurance, even though the beneficiary at the moment was his dog.

He wanted to tell Deke to call another agency, or call State Farm back and talk to somebody more experienced.

Still, he kept silent. He was on the team, but not one of the team yet. Those were two different rungs of a special ladder. He had more climbing to do.

Hondo came into the locker room just as Street was working himself up to actually saying something. They all watched as he crossed to the supply closet, which had "Ladies' Locker Room" taped on the door, and he knocked.

Sanchez opened the closet door, stuffing her uniform into a duffel bag.

"On your headshot," Hondo said, "you got to hit the vermilion line every time."

"Yes, sir. Got it."

He moved off, and T.J., Boxer, and Deke followed him out of the locker room. Street watched them go.

Christine Sanchez sidled over to Street, keeping her voice low just in case it carried through the tiled room. "What's a verwhatchit line?" she asked quietly.

"Vermilion line. It's where you drool. You drool much in public?"

"Try not to."

"You hit a guy between his gums and eyebrows, he's going down. Doesn't matter if there's a gun in his hand, finger on the trigger, he's not getting a shot off. Brain can't send the message to his trigger."

"What's it called again? Ver—"

"Just call it the drool line."

"Drool line I can remember."

She thanked him with a glance and strode outside, probably to join the others. He wanted to go too, though he held back.

Come on, get over it. You're not in high school!

By the time he had his running shoes on, he had convinced himself that he needed more to go to the gym than to chase after the clique he wanted to be in. Had to resist that teenager reaction, even though he felt like one right now. Back on S.W.A.T.!

Then it hit him. Something had been bothering him ever since Hondo told him he was back on. Well, two things. One, he didn't really believe the choice wouldn't be rescinded at the top. Two, he wanted to call Brian and give him some good news.

Wouldn't that turn sour fast? Still, he had the reaction. It was like always wanting to call somebody who had died and just hear his voice again. Dead's dead. You can't just pick up a phone.

Where was he? What was he doing? He wasn't dead, Street knew, and in some ways that was worse. Brian had gone out on a bad note, an ugly and insincere moment of vicious resentment, the kind of moment most people spend their lives trying to avoid. He wasn't dead, he was out there somewhere, probably working, unable to do the work he was really cut out for. It was like having legs and never being allowed to walk.

"Rest of the team's going to grab a beer. I'm buying."

Street buried a flinch and turned. Hondo stood in the doorway, holding on to the doorjamb and not exactly coming inside.

"You can buy me two after we pass," Street told him. "Gotta hit the gym."

Now Hondo did come in, and kept his voice between the two of them.

Probably the others were still outside. Sure they were—waiting for Hondo.

"Fuller's not gonna make it easy for us," Hondo told him with abrupt confidentiality. This was the first time he'd admitted he couldn't have his way just by bullying. "Captain Fuller's throwing everything he has at me. I figure that's okay. Then we'll be ready for pretty much anything this city can cough up. Fuller's waiting for you to trip, you or me, and so far we haven't."

But what was the real message? Was there something he thought Street could do to butter the way? He tried to think of something he hadn't already done, short of sending Fuller flowers.

"Good," he said. "I'd hate to break a sweat just for a first round knockout."

"Big day tomorrow," Hondo told him. "Save

some strength for it. Don't burn all you got at the gym."

"I got plenty."

"You were ready for this test after the first day," Hondo agreed. "Team's going to be relying on you out there."

Was that a warning?

"I'll cover my end," Street said. Then he paused and added, "Can I ask you something?"

"Of course."

"Why'd you pick me?"

He braced himself for the answer, and hoped he would be up to the expectation, whatever it was.

Hondo contemplated the question for a moment. His lips twisted into a grin. "I knew it'd piss off the captain."

He was still thinking about that conversation the next morning at the training site parking lot. He was twenty-five minutes early, late for him, but getting to be about normal for the others. His chronic earliness had caused a tectonic movement under the rest of the team. Now everybody came early.

Sanchez was here already too. The others would be driving up any minute. Sanchez sat outside her car, cross-legged on the pavement, enjoying the early sunlight over the mountains.

What was she doing? Street paused and watched, then just crossed over to her.

Oh—she was taping a picture of her daughter to her vest.

Street decided not to make a smart remark. Might be taken wrong, and he didn't want to alienate his only friend on earth.

Whoa, are we a little paranoid, Jimmy?

"You forgot your radio codes," he said, and leaned down to tape those to her wrist, right where she could read them easily.

"Thanks," she said, and blushed a little at letting her sentimentality get ahead of the need for support contact.

By the time he got back to his own car, Boxer and T.J. arrived in the same vehicle and got out. Boxer was just finishing wrapping his hands like— well, like a boxer.

"We'll try not to slow you down out there, hotshot," he said unkindly to Street.

T.J. added, "And if we screw up, try not to tell on us."

The insult burned.

Street felt his innards shrink into knots. Was there anything he could say? Anger would be taken—

The scream of tires slashed his thought and rescued him from having to respond, or not respond. He spun around to see the team's black Suburban squawk to a stop. Hondo stuck his head out of the driver's window.

"Come on! We got the call!"

9

MOJAVE SITE

THE SUBURBAN CRESTED A RIDGE WITH STREET AT THE wheel. Hondo and the others were using the time to gear up and psych up.

In the deep foreground lay a half-crushed L-1011 with its wings sheared off, surrounded by a collection of L.A.P.D. sedans and other S.W.A.T. vehicles already on the site. A dozen officers and special-tactics team members hovered about, including Captain Fuller in a red baseball cap, consulting with several sergeants and other officers of various levels.

"Here's the scenario," Hondo explained, just below an excited shout. "Three hijackers, armed with handguns and knives, control that aircraft. They've killed a hostage and have threatened to kill the rest unless fuel and a pilot are provided in the hour. The red hats on board are senior staff sergeants and will be grading you. S.W.A.T. officers will be playing the roles of the hostages. Some S.W.A.T. officers will be playing the roles of the terrorists and trying to kill you."

"They want us to fail?" Boxer asked.

"Actually, they do. We're not going to oblige them."

Street listened with heightening passion to the instructions and the details.

He remembered this. It was the most unpleasant experience of his life the first time. At every other point everybody else wanted a trainee to succeed. At this point they were all out to get you, to kill you, destroy you, prove you couldn't do the job, and they were serious.

Just thinking about the final exam for the Special Weapons and Tactics duty had almost made him not want to come back, but every second thought buried the first.

Now that he was here, though . . . his stomach was not happy at all.

His arms and legs ached from tension. They were all out to get everybody on the team, but they were especially out to get Jim Street, the rat, the tattle, the traitor. He had friends on the force, yet had spent six months enduring the doubts and uncertainties that were of his own making.

He'd never been much of a talker, and even his friends weren't that clear on his background or his philosophies. Even the ones who didn't quite believe he had turned on Brian Gamble would be double out to get him today. They wanted to know just how right or wrong they might be.

Within four minutes Hondo was leaning on the hood of the Suburban, spreading out a diagram of the aircraft fuselage out there. They didn't have much time. In reality they wouldn't have it and no one would let them have it now.

"There are two dynamic entry points," Hondo instructed. "Here, through the forward landing gear . . . and back here, through the luggage hatch. Captain's gonna have guys sitting ambush at points. We get hung up, we're done."

Done? Back to square one? Or all of them disbanded from the elite team and Hondo gone, and somebody else trying to put together a whole new group? Even without asking, Street heard the answer ring in his head. This was a one-chance deal.

"Hondo," he spoke up quickly, thinking fast, "there's another way in."

At first they didn't believe him, though in seconds their desire for an edge turned in his favor. Boxer and T.J. moved aside while Street pointed at the diagram and had them follow his finger.

"There's an elevator here that brings up the serving carts. There's a mechanic's access here."

"I've known a few stewardesses."

"Just a few?" Sanchez teased, with a hint of respect for the knowledge if not the romance.

Hondo squinted at the itty-bitty mark on the sketch of the plane. "How many men can we fit up this thing?"

"None."

Annoyance only lasted a little while before they understood. They made their plan in mere seconds, then moved out smartly. Single file, the team crept toward the plane. Deke and Boxer ran out in the open, in plain sight, then took cover behind a service vehicle. The others used that same diversion to get underneath the plane.

Street had a terrible feeling of being watched while he opened the small hatch in the rear wheel well of the plane. Of course, he *was* being watched, though not by the people in the plane. The officers inside, pretending to be victims and terrorists, had no idea what was going on, no more than real victims or terrorists would. They wouldn't even have been told the exercise had commenced.

The more spontaneous this encounter could be, the better for all involved.

But it was strange. The S.W.A.T. team was obliged to do everything by the book, within the law, yet were also expected to think outside the common perimeters and be creative, surprising, *if* they could figure out how to do it without compromising the force, which stood in the unforgiving and uncomplimentary glare of public opinion.

Those lines were pretty fine.

Might be a good thing, the idea that even cops couldn't get away with stretching the law very much anymore. The days of the corrupt Chicago P.D. or the freewheeling totalitarian county sheriff who executed his enemies for their gambling debts had waned with the coming of cop cameras and cell phones, not to mention a wiser general public.

How things were in the wilds of Appalachia, he had no way to know, but here in civilization, things were generally better. Any cop who couldn't deal with being under constant scrutiny had better find another line of work.

He was determined not to be one of those. He would do his job as well as he could, make his judgment calls, and deal with the repercussions—just as he had that day in the bank, which had ultimately landed him here, for his great second chance.

Or last chance.

He tried to bury those thoughts, but they piled on top of the tension and the nerves and kept recurring.

The hatch dropped open in his hands, barely fourteen inches square. Street could've gotten everything but his shoulders in. T.J., maybe a leg.

Sanchez, though, shimmied inside and wriggled her way up the access hatch. Dangerous—she'd had to strip out of much of her protective equipment in order to get inside, and when she came out the top, she would be vulnerable.

Street hoped the people inside hadn't been given schematics of the plane, or hadn't known to do their homework. That was the mystery, wasn't it? How much did the bad guys know? What were their strengths? Their gaps of intelligence and surveillance, or forethought or preparation?

These weren't terrorists, though. They were cops. Street allowed himself to know what he could know about them. That was an edge, and he had it. They would be able to anticipate the team's moves, understand their training, and know what was expected.

He heard a click. Sanchez! She had unbolted the door and was using the light on her M-4 to see as she removed the door and set it aside. Street played it in his mind, ticking off the seconds and pacing out each move she would have to make.

She would be climbing up the elevator shaft now. More room, and more chance of being heard.

Street's hands started to sweat and tingle in empathy. He gripped his weapon tighter.

He counted off ten seconds, then moved to the other aft entry door, the one they would be expected to blow.

So he would blow it, nice and loud. He attached some plastique to the door, doing what he would have to do in the real world—guessing about the amount.

Boxer would be opening the other hatch, the luggage door, right about now, in another predictable move—*pop*. There it was.

If Street had heard it, the hijackers sure would. They would be signaling each other now . . . getting into position to attack the barnstormers. They would be lingering in key places, glancing at each other, ticking off seconds, holding their own weapons at ready.

Would they have rifles? Handguns? Box cutters?

Street made a mental bet with himself. There would be either knives or handguns, or both. Probably nothing more creative than that. Maybe some pepper spray or CS gas. He decided to be ready for that, no matter how unlikely it might be that anyone but he was twisted enough to keep a pocket full of that stuff for a situation like this.

Terrorists were out to kill and, well, to terrorize, not to warn or just debilitate.

He slipped inside, into the guts of the airplane.

He knew Hondo, Velasquez, and Fuller would be watching the operation behind a glass partition and twitched a little at how weird that was. The idea that this could be a fair test was just wishful thinking. The real tests always came in the street, with truly unpredictable opponents. Today was almost like a formality that could knock them completely down before they ever got to the tests that mattered, out there, in the raw open metropolis.

He held his breath, but that only made him dizzy, and then he had to breathe all the harder. He forced himself to breathe evenly, though he couldn't help breathing too deeply.

In, out . . . in . . . out . . . listen . . . listen . . . in, out . . .

A whiff of detonated plastique.

He was inside the main compartment now, after some shimmying. He felt T.J. pressed in behind him, being careful not to push. Street nudged a tiny inspection mirror out from the stainless-steel cabinetry from which his little entryway emerged. In the dentistry-size reflector he spotted two hijackers, one by the galley area, next to the lavatory, the other—

BAM! Sanchez!

She was in the main compartment! She took out the guy near the galley. Suddenly there was a flurry of motion and there were hijackers heading toward the rear of the plane. Flashbang grenades started going off in two separate areas, and suddenly the air was filled with gray-white smoke.

The side hatch blew open, throwing a blast of heat and small bits of metal and insulation that refused to settle, but just floated around glittering. Flashbangs exploded in three severe cracks immediately after, pumping more smoke and confusion. Sanchez provided cover while Deke and Boxer stormed in, making use of the gusts of smoke and debris.

Another bust of paintgun fire came from Sanchez as she took down a guy near the emergency exit, hiding among the passengers. Street dived back to the left aisle, tucked and rolled, and came up shooting at a perp who was hiding in the galley. Blue paint sprayed across the lateral bulkhead and all over the guy, mostly in the head and chest.

The good shot caused a problem—it gave a fourth man a chance to take Street from behind, so very close that all Street could do was duck.

T.J. barreled up the aisle to point-blank range

and opened fire on the hijacker about to lay Street out like a lamb in the slaughterhouse. In a haze of blue spray Street scampered out of the way and let T.J. have his kill, but that put him in an unscouted position, and sure enough somebody was there to take advantage of it.

More a sensation, instinct, than actual sight, Street caught an idea of somebody on his right and ducked for another roll along the aisle. He came up aimed, but this time his gun was pointed at an innocent passenger, a woman who—

No, it wasn't! The "passenger" sprang up with a machine gun, ready to spray the whole forward cabin.

Street nailed the woman in the midsection before her paintgun could go off. He dived back into the aisle right over her head as she did her job playing dead, and straightened to find a paintpistol right in his face.

No, past his face. It was Deke, and he aimed right past Street's ear at a hijacker who was holding a girl hostage by the throat.

Pokpokpok Deke didn't wait. The hijacker was hit right in the neck. Ouch—paint or not.

The remaining hijackers were caught between them and Street and T.J. The S.W.A.T. team had dispersed perfectly, reading one another's minds, covering both of the airplane's aisles and covering one another without getting in the wrong lines of fire.

Street and T.J. didn't wait for applause. They

rushed the remaining hijackers, simunitions popping like movie-theater snacks. When Street noticed that Sanchez was cornered, he jockeyed sideways as if on a skateboard, left his position, and took out the hijacker who had her pinned.

He hit the poor slob a little too hard too. *Getting lost in the role, Jim?*

He couldn't congratulate himself. He had saved Sanchez, but T.J. had been left without cover and taken a blast to the chest from the other hijacker. This was reality practice.

Street got a clump of lead deep in his gut—he'd lost his partner.

T.J. grimaced at the hard smack in the chest, shook his head in frustration, and went to his knee reluctantly. Deke returned fire, though, and the assailant had to admit he was down too.

"Clear!" Street shouted.

"Clear!" Deke.

Boxer, somewhere behind Street, called, "Clear!"

"Clear," Sanchez said, not so loudly.

Hondo, over a radio, confirmed, "Ten-David, Seventy-David, Code Four. We're all clear."

Then Hondo grinned at his team. The hostages, all alive, seemed impressed, and so were the various red hats posted through the cabin. They knew before their next breath that they had beaten the record by the clock.

Still annoyed at himself, Street didn't dare glance at T.J. Instead he stuck his hand out to the "dead" guy he'd just slammed and gave him a thankful grip.

"Good job," the guy said. "Look at Fuller's face. You guys made it."

Street turned and looked at the glass partition. Captain Fuller wasn't meeting anybody's eyes. He didn't enjoy anything about this success. Said a lot about him.

Aw, hell.

He turned to T.J. and reached out to help him up.

T.J. didn't accept the help. He turned halfway away from Street and fiddled with his weapon.

"McCabe," Street prodded. He had cover— everybody else was trying to get out of the smoky plane, picking up weapons, shells, each other. "Sorry."

"For what?"

"Just sorry, okay?"

"Oh—" T.J. looked up. "You mean for ditching me for Sanchez?"

Ouch. "Yeah. It was just instinct. I've got to fight it."

"Yeah. Well . . ." T.J. shifted on his feet.

"No, don't cut me any slack. Nobody ever has. Why should you be first?"

"I won't, don't worry."

"I can't get over the girl thing. I just jumped to protect her. Never even gave Deke and Boxer a chance, and they were over there. Swear to God, I'll fight it from now on."

T.J. picked at the smear of paint on his chest, which otherwise could be blood. "I got my vest on. I could take a blow like this." He looked up at Street. "Maybe I'm not dead."

Street stood back. "Are you shitting me? Are you—"

"Cutting you slack? Yeah, I guess I am."

"I should choke myself before I ask, but . . . why?"

T.J. shifted again and actually blushed. "Because I was about to do the same thing to you. You just beat me to it."

Street leaned closer. "Hey, maybe we got a loophole here."

"You mean like, if two of us were about to do it, maybe it's not the major fuckup it looked like?"

"Yeah! Maybe!"

"Deal!"

They laughed, swore in their heads that they would fight to view Sanchez as just another S.W.A.T. officer and never do this again, even though they were probably both lying to themselves. The instinct to protect a woman was deeply wired and would take probably months to pound down, training or not.

Then again, the instinct to protect each other, male or female, had been in play too. Some things didn't look right in retrospect, even though they had to be acted upon in split seconds. It was another one of those moments for Street. At least this one had happened in a training maneuver and not in a bank with real blood and real bullets.

Learn, boy, learn. Grow.

Basking in T.J.'s forgiveness, Street was the last one out of the ravaged fuselage. He came down the gangway to the cheers and backslapping of people he would've sworn hated his guts. He didn't know what had changed over the past days, yet there was a definite difference.

He had stubbornly held to a dream, endured humiliation and personal torment. It seemed as if they all realized that at this particular minute and were willing to finally give him the benefit of personal growth. Their doubts were suspended for now, and everyone here was willing to put his—or her—life in Jim Street's hands.

Now all he had to do was make sure he never screwed up again for the rest of his life and the life everlasting.

Easy.

LEO'S RIBS

"Sir, you are the true master!"

Boxer reached up and took a plateful of steaming ribs from Deke's dad, Leo Kaye. Deke appeared behind his father with a second plate, also piled high, and took a seat next to Street.

"Thank you, sir," Mr. Kaye said with a bow. "I've never heard Deke talk about anyone as much as he talks about all of you."

"Please, Pop," Deke warned, but too late.

Sanchez laughed and Boxer clapped Deke sympathetically on the back.

"My boy's grown up, huh?"

The older man tapped a row of family pictures

pegged to the wall, pointing to one very funny overweight kid with a huge—now, really, huge—ball of afro.

"Deke . . ." Sanchez eyed the photo. "Dude, is that you?"

"Yep. Papa nailed 'em up so I can't take 'em down."

"You were a serious butterball!" Boxer charged.

"All in the past."

Boxer took that as a warning and turned his attention to his ribs. "Wish my wife cooked like this!"

"C'mon, Deke," Sanchez allowed. "Dig in."

"That's all right. I'm cool." And he pulled out a tuna sandwich, which he began quietly to eat with they all looked in wonderment.

"Deke," T.J. began, "that's just *wrong*."

Boxer wagged a rib. "These are amazing!"

"I know they're amazing," Deke admitted. "I worked here every summer! Turned me into Fat Albert. Eatin' right turned me into this."

He stood up, pulled up his shirt, and revealed his killer washboard.

The team whooped and cheered for him.

"Sell it, Deke, sell it!" Sanchez chortled.

Deke started dancing—and, damn him, he wasn't bad.

Jim Street watched and listened to all this, having hardly said a word since they arrived. He just didn't want to blow the feeling of finally having won.

Now he finally leaned back and started to relax,

to enjoy himself, sensing that he was more at home here than he had been anywhere in a long time. Even Boxer had suspended the resentment for now. People got together and then broke up. Life.

"I forgot to bring tip money!" he wailed as Deke gyrated like a cross between Michael Jackson and Jackie Chan.

"Celebrating, I see."

It was Hondo, just arriving. Deke immediately pulled his shirt down and got serious, more or less. This was it.

Street noticed a look of strain on Hondo's face and wondered what could have gone wrong, and yet he knew. The situation had been so controlled during the final, yet was supposed to be something it could never really be—random. Budget, equipment, and imagination were the limiting factors, and there were only so many variations on a theme that could be enacted on a drill field.

The human element was also a kind of limiting factor. Cops had plenty of experience, but they weren't exactly artists or playwrights. They were men and women who dealt in hardware and its use, not musicians trying to trying to find a melody that would inspire anyone.

They all had stories in them, but few were storytellers. Police officers designed the courses and did their best to confound each other, but there was always the absence of that random maniacal element—desperation and self-preservation, consciencelessness

and true evil intent, which dominated any actual **crime scene.** Only bad guys in a situation gone bad could bring up the real level that would test the team's mettle.

Everybody sat up straight as Hondo joined them, but pretended not to, and hit their nerves in pretending to keep eating.

Luckily, with food like this, burying your fears was easy, easy, easy.

Unfortunately, there still had to be a debriefing. They all had a pretty good idea how it would go. They had fixated not on their win, really, but on the loss of one of their team. Even in practice, that was hard to forget.

Everything was too close to real. Just a drill, sure. This time it was just a drill.

"Hell, yeah, we're celebrating," Sanchez said, the only one of them with the nerve to push the moment forward.

"And you should be," Hondo told them sincerely. "It was a kick-ass display. But let's remember one thing. If this was a real operation, not a test, one of us would be calling T.J.'s family right now, trying to explain what went wrong."

Street felt himself shrink.

He tried not to look at T.J, but couldn't help a glance. T.J. was looking down at the table, both ashamed and disturbed. Indeed there was such a thing as too close for comfort.

"One casualty," Hondo said, "may be acceptable by department standards. It's never acceptable by

mine. So celebrate tonight. But tomorrow . . . we're
S.W.A.T."

Hondo's home was Spartan and industrial, like
the sweeping hills outside. There was workout
equipment, some furniture, a wooden striking tree
for hardening up those fists and forearms. Jim
Street looked around, wondering where the sink
and the john were, or if Hondo just held it.

"This is like seeing Bruce Lee's lair," he murmured.

"Yeah. I don't need much."

Hondo led the way to an old refrigerator that
after fifty years was now back in style. Street
peeked around and noted that the inside of the
fridge was perfectly organized with meals in Tupperware and bottles of juice and organics in tidy
rows. Now, here was a side of Hondo he wouldn't
have bet on.

Hondo poured a couple of shots, but not
whiskey. Wheatgrass juice. Back in training.

"C'mon." He led the way through a sliding door
onto a nicely appointed balcony with some plants
and a nice rural view.

The night air had taken on a brisk coolness since
they left the street, or maybe it was just from being
up on a hill. The building wasn't too tall, but provided a great view of downtown Los Angeles in the
distance, on the other side of some really precious
hills. The city wore its jewelry all the time, and now
looked like a necklace on the hills' shoulders.

Beyond that, earrings of stars topped the miles and miles of urban glitter.

All of L.A. had buildings that were created to be looked at. Very different from places like New York or Baltimore, cities that had grown organically, Los Angeles was like a big billboard or a cluster of decorator showplaces, built area by area out of wealth and a firm knowledge that the future was coming in a certain way, with a lot of money.

The fast-growing movie industry back in the elegant and hustling thirties had chosen the Hollywood area because of its notoriously consistent sunny weather and reasonable temperature almost every day of the year. Budgets could be planned, completion dates etched in, and business could stand a pretty good chance of not being confounded by storms.

Of course, there was never snow, and even the rain would soon go away. Being right on the ocean and flanked by mountains on the other side, Los Angeles never had a storm stall overhead to confound some poor director trying to make a distribution date for yet another TV movie or independent film, or even the big industry blockbusters. Give or take smog, every day was dependably lovely.

Sadly, that meant crime never took a day off. There were no winter chills to keep perpetrators inside, no downtime for muggers or robbers or the otherwise cold-blooded among us. Days were pleasant, nights warm, mornings foggy and mysterious. California opened her sun-drenched expanses to all comers, good and, unfortunately, bad.

And the sprawling city itself, with all its adjoining cities and settled neighborhoods, from the barrios to the plush velvety lawns and mansions of the super-rich, were sparkled with sand-colored architecture and tropical foliage sculpted into perfect form, and coleus bushes the size of trucks. Those bushes were only houseplants in most of the rest of the country, give or take maybe Texas and Florida.

Greater Los Angeles knew it was being looked at and had been built that way. Even the bad neighborhoods benefited when someone wanted to make a film there, and changes were accordingly made. Every young architect who wanted to make his mark came to the Southern California cityscape to make it, and thus every building, street, cul-de-sac, and restaurant was somebody's piece of artwork, someone's way of making a statement in this world and making sure he wasn't completely forgotten. Many built careers on getting the smallest chance to show off here.

There was a lot of money in the L.A. sphere, and every dollar moved down to employ more and more people from all walks of life, until there were chances for a pretty good life here for anybody who wanted to work. From Disneyland to Universal, to the hundreds of restaurants and shops serving a huge and privileged population, anybody who wanted to work could find some kind of work here and build a life.

They might not all be rich, but they would all be warm in winter and have food from a sparkling supermarket, and most would have cars and TVs. If you had TV, you were doing okay. The quality of your life was up to you.

Yet, enormous clusters of people meant a certain percentage of scavengers, bottom-feeders, lazy users, and opportunistic abusers who wrecked things for everyone else. Not a big percentage, but enough to stain a place that would otherwise be paradise.

Street tried to imagine living anywhere else, one of those small towns in America, places that sounded like mythological grottoes in comparison to L.A. He had never been outside of L.A. except during his turn in the Navy, and somehow that didn't really count. The service controlled the lives of its soldiers, and you were protected in so many ways that really living in another place was different from serving there.

He made a mental note to visit America some day, to cross those mountains and see what went on in the towns he knew must be out there, places where Andy and Barney could solve all the problems of crime and punishment in an hour.

Was that real? Could there be places where he could leave his car unlocked and tell his neighbors to just go on inside the house if they needed to?

Maybe a nice vacation, but what would he do for excitement if there were no hostage situations?

"You surprised Fuller, y'know." Hondo startled him out of his thoughts. "He figured you'd go with

Gamble. Become a desperado. He never thought you'd stick it out."

Street took a couple of seconds to distill that.

"S.W.A.T.'s home for me. I have to get back in the house. Never thought you'd be the one to let me in."

"Me neither," Hondo admitted. "You have a bad kill, they lock me up because I picked you for a second chance. But hell . . . I gotta tell you, if I was in your shoes, I would've done the same damned thing in that bank."

Street felt a kind of shadow come down over his face. "The negotiator wasn't inside. Nobody was but me and Gamble. It was gonna be a bloodbath."

Sirens sounded deep in the distance. The two men automatically perked up like fire horses hearing the bell.

An ambulance and a fire engine approached from the north, then turned west and headed on toward the residential area in the valley. Men and women at work, helping the city stay civilized. The sirens squawled boldly, then faded into the depths of lower California.

"All I got is S.W.A.T.," Street said. "I thought it would be enough to get back on. Now . . . to tell you the truth . . . I'm kind of scared."

Hondo actually smiled, but warmly, as if he knew that feeling. "Know what you mean. Just don't get so busy saving everyone else that you forget to save yourself."

Street gazed at him gratefully. A tiny buzzing

sensation ran up his arms, as if Hondo had just passed him a torch. He knew he would have a whole new mystery to ponder for the next plenty of days. Training was over. They had passed. They were a team, an elite unit upon whom everyone else would depend. They were the last line of defense—the first line of offense.

Whatever happened to them after tomorrow would be real life, and real death if things turned sour.

LOS ANGELES COUNTY JAIL

A sea of blue jumpsuits, bright blue. Eight incarcerated men.

Alex Lupin sat among them, being bound over for trial for whatever they had drummed up.

They still didn't realize who he was. The fake ID had done its job. They would be weeks tracking down the very efficient paper trail laid behind him. The unreal person whose name he was using even had a history in Europe that would lead the computers on a merry chase through three nations before striking a brick wall.

"Dude, I hate this place," the man next to him said, a pathetic soul with whom a king would never sit unless he meant to create an illusion. "I never been so scared in my whole life."

They sat together in a corner of the prison yard, opening bag lunches. Sandwiches. Cheese and apples.

"What do they say you did?" Lupin asked.

"Tagging."

"Writing on walls?"

"Yeah. Just to get my name out there. The fame game." The man shuddered and picked his teeth with a plastic knife.

Before Lupin could comment, two large Hispanics, probably gang members, crossed toward them. He had heard about the gangs here in L.A. These two were shaking down the prison yard for other people's lunches.

"Gimme your apple, dog," the bigger one said to Tagger.

The second was not looking at Lupin's sandwich. "You too homeboy. Kick down, bitch."

Lupin raised his eyes from the man's sizable thighs to his unpleasant face. "Go away."

Lupin was not a large man, but this he had learned many years ago and had made a plan to compensate. A man of his means could afford the best of everything.

It took a beat for the insult to process. These two Hispanics were not used to being resisted in a place they considered to be theirs by right of power. But Lupin ruled entire countries, under all the tables.

The second gang member swung at him, a clumsy and untidy move that left his armpit open for assault. Lupin slipped down and brought his hard-toed shoe up into the man's armpit, then drove the heel into his ribs. The man stumbled. When he recovered, Lupin exploded into a torrent of strikes. In less than five seconds the gangster lay destroyed in a puddle of blood from his own nose. He moaned, insensible, as

Lupin delivered a series of kicks to the groin, throat, and nose of the first man, who would never on this day get anybody else's apple.

The best of everything . . . including martial arts lessons. Lupin had even starred in two movies, made by his own companies.

Under assumed names, of course. All he wanted was to show off. The fame didn't matter. He just liked to play.

But this was more fun. He didn't have to worry about how much he was paying the stuntmen.

In a final flourish he drove a heel into his opponent's thigh, and grinned as the bone cracked. The man went down, howling.

Lupin picked up the Tagger's apple and handed it back to him. There was a commotion, then, on the other side of the yard. Guards, probably.

No one met Lupin's eyes as he quietly sat back down and picked up his own sandwich.

The prisoners parted like the Red Sea as deputies with helmets and clubs charged into the open area. But no one was resisting, so the deputies only made warning movements.

"Transport these inmates to the infirmary," one of them said to the others. "No fighting in the module! I put the smack down in here, not you assholes! Who did this?"

Lupin leaned against the cool brick wall and took a bite out of his sandwich.

The Tagger stood up. "Sir, they just started thumping on each other, sir."

The other prisoners paused, then some of them nodded.

"That's right."

"Just went after each other."

"Something about a woman."

"His mother."

"Yeah. Mothersomethin'."

And then there was laughter.

Alex Lupin laughed too, but not for the same reason.

The guards knew it wasn't true, but what could they do about it? They had no idea what had really happened, and Lupin had been careful to be sitting in one of very few areas where the surveillance cameras really couldn't see around the corner of this wall. He had scouted the location for days. It was his private corner now, whenever he needed it.

"Yeah. Everybody inside. Outdoor privileges are over for the day."

The head guard motioned, and everyone started filing toward the prison interior again.

"You," the guard said, pointing at Lupin. "Your lawyer's here again."

Lupin stood up. "Ah. Thank you so much, Officer, for your kind attention."

"Get the hell inside."

"Again, thank you."

"I've been patient all day, Kathy. Day after day. What's going on?

Alex Lupin sat with his pretty lawyer and imagined what she would look like if she were not so pretty anymore. He played with her facial features and imagined what he would tell her if he didn't like what she told him today. He would describe her future to her and see if things changed. This dawdling was becoming intolerable. Didn't she know how to use the resources she had at her fingertips? Money? Contacts? Threats? Influence? Politicians?

"This is the problem." She kept her voice low. "Your prints don't match your ID. They're running another check right now through the FBI and Interpol."

"Interpol!" he spat. He leaned forward and growled, "Get . . . me . . . out of here."

"I'm doing everything I can!" A fine sweat broke out on her powdered brow.

"Do more. This is easy. Who do I pay?"

"You can't solve this problem by throwing money at—"

"Then who do I have to *kill*?"

"Hey . . . I'm talking to the judge," she protested, "pulling favors . . . wait till Monday."

"No, Kathy. We need to do something. Now."

10

"WHAT'S WRONG WITH YOU PEOPLE! IT'S ONLY ELEVEN! I've got a baby-sitter for the first time in three months!"

Sanchez chased Deke and Boxer out to the parking lot, followed by Street and T.J. Hondo was already gone, racing away to do paperwork to solidify the new elite team before anybody with a chip on his shoulder could botch the deal or start pulling on any loose threads.

"We've been up since four," Deke told her.

"That's weak," she challenged.

"I'm back home before midnight, I got a shot at getting some."

"T.J.?"

T.J. just grinned from his driver's seat. "I get home before midnight, I *know* I'm getting some."

"Boxer?"

"I know I'm not getting any, but my wife'll still want me home."

Sanchez groaned and swung around to Street,

and, though he knew he was not her first choice, she got him in a neck lock and wailed, "You know how hard it is to get a baby-sitter?"

Street glanced around as the parking lot rapidly emptied around them.

"It's not brain surgery, Street!" Sanchez howled. "I'm offering to buy you a drink!"

Ten minutes later they were at Street's favorite beach pub, doing everything they could to make sure they knew this was not, not, not a date, and that everybody else knew it too.

After all, Street wanted a chance eventually at courting and conquering every one of the statuesque women prowling the pub.

Sanchez, not nearly as well sculpted as much of the goddesses who circled them now, looked around without even pretending she wasn't looking around.

"What's the deal with all these hotties?" she bluntly asked, clinging to a Guana Grabber in a tall frosted glass.

"This is where the flight attendants come," he told her. "LAX is right around the corner."

"And you come here to provide police service to the aviation industry, I suppose.'

"First time here, actually."

He cupped his hands around a dish of beer nuts and stirred it absently with a little umbrella.

"Yo, Jimmy!" The waitress showed up with beer and a couple of shots of tequila. "Did you pass?"

Street felt his cheeks flush. Completely forgot about Angelica.

He just nodded.

Angelica took his bill and ripped it up. "Awesome! It's on the house!"

Sanchez just eyed him, but she seemed to have known all along that he was full of manure on most things and that somehow he wasn't all the rage he wanted people to think he was when it came to women.

Well, he wasn't, okay?

Sure, there had been plenty of girls, and they were easy come and easy go in California, especially for a young cop in good physical shape who could surf. The formula was good for Jim Street, and still he felt empty most of the time. He got more love from his dog and more attention from his job.

He had made a couple of sincere attempts, which he'd thought at the time had been well considered, at long-range relationships and even saw himself happily married in the bubble of future wishes in his head. That formula, though, hadn't come up yet. He didn't know how to do it the way other men did, like tell the difference between love and sex, or understand what long-range really meant, with all the downs and bumps and stresses that made a relationship worth hanging on to over years upon years.

Maybe that was what Boxer had been so mad about where his sister was concerned. Maybe

Street had given her the idea that he meant to stay together for a long time, then just couldn't manage to keep the emotional stamina going. She'd tried. He had too, but it was like he'd been running for months and his legs just finally gave out.

Still, he wanted that some day.

Was it true what they said about the "right" girl? What the romantics and the stories insisted was true?

"No tequila," Sanchez said.

Had only a second or two gone by?

"I have a kid to get home to," Sanchez went on. "Be here all night behind that shit."

So Street did both shots. Somehow he suddenly needed a good brain blast. Then he turned to her and they bumped beers in mutual congratulations.

"So how do you juggle work and a daughter?" he asked.

She paused, thought about it, then shrugged. "I don't do anything else. My mom helps with Eliza. You find a way to make it work. What about you?"

"Me?"

"Beside S.W.A.T., what are you juggling? Waitresses or flight attendants?"

He shrugged dramatically. "I try not to limit myself."

She smirked. Her dark eyes and dark hair made her look suddenly exotic and clever among all these blondes and surfer-types. She was a real woman, not a synthetic one. All of a sudden, that mattered. Until now he'd always gone for plastic.

"Real humanitarian," she droned.

Street thought about keeping up the illusion of Prince à la Beach, but ended up ditching the attitude. She was going to be one of his partners from now on. If he was going to impress her, he wanted it to be honest and the real him.

"Nah," he said. "I can't seem to juggle even one girl these days, let alone three or four."

"Let me guess. The longest relationship you've ever had is with your cat."

"Dog. Four years this Christmas."

"Happy anniversary."

She bumped his beer again, and they took a pause for a long draw.

"We did good work today, huh?" she asked then.

He nodded, but made no comments about the specifics of the operation. He didn't want to think of T.J.'s "death" or lie to himself that T.J. might have been just injured. He couldn't get that one very far. Terrorists knew about Kevlar and would be ready for it. Armor-piercers.

Just the impact at that range could've killed him.

Quit trying to lie to yourself. It won't change anything. Lying never really does.

"What's it like?"

Sanchez's voice pushed him out of his worries. He looked at her, and for a moment he didn't know what she meant.

"Oh," he uttered. "It's faster. A lot faster. You never get a chance . . . to . . ."

His words trailed off, not interrupted, but just

fading. He was looking across the beach pub to the pool table, hazy from smoke and cluttered with slow-moving people watching a game. The game had temporarily stopped, and almost everyone was just standing there, looking.

"Know that guy?" Sanchez followed his gaze through the pub to a strong young man with five o'clock shadow and dangerous eyes.

"Used to," Street choked up.

By now the man and another one were on their way across the pub, through the crowd, many of whom had noticed there was something going on. They didn't care, but they noticed. Local pub soap operas were always fun for the partially drunk.

Without being aware until it was too late, Street found himself shaking hands with the five o'clock shadow.

"How are you?" he asked, and he meant it.

"Okay," Brian Gamble said as though he mostly meant what he said too. "Time's my own. Do whatever I want . . . don't take orders from no one."

Street tried to think of something to say. He'd spent six months imagining what he'd say to Gamble if he ever ran into him. The list of possible topics and regrets and disagreements and sorries was overbearing, and now he couldn't think of a single one.

So he said, "Congratulations."

Gamble's eyes were hard, despite his words. "And congratulations to you. I heard they took you back."

How could he have heard so fast? The final was just today. Could word really spread that quickly? Or had he been paying attention to Street's career all these months?

Maybe Brian was not so far out of circulation as he pretended.

"Your girlfriend?" He eyed Sanchez.

"No," Street said. "She's S.W.A.T."

Gamble's faced flushed with something between anger and surprise. "This what it's come to? Bustin' down doors with J-Lo? I didn't know they made bulletproof tampons."

Well, this was going nicely.

Street started to say something, to try backing off, but Sanchez was already in Gamble's face.

"They make bulletproof condoms for that prick of yours?" she tossed back.

"Ooooh," Gamble responded. "She talks a good game."

Street reached out a few inches and pulled Sanchez out of the line of fire. This was too much.

He eyed the other guy, the one who until now had only tagged behind Gamble. "Out on the town with your girlfriend, Curly Sue?"

"No," the other guy said, "but you can be my bitch."

Ah, a sophisticate. Gamble had obviously fallen in with an uptown crowd and learned good manners.

"Do I get benefits with that? Or just the satisfaction of sending you flying across that table?"

The guy sidled up to Street, and they eyed each other without a flinch. Gamble, though, knew perfectly well what Street could do—more than most—and warned, "Leave it alone, Travis."

What had begun with a handshake and a touch of potential suddenly dissolved into acrimony. Gamble grinned and pushed his companion out of the way, back toward the pool table.

"Glad all your dicksucking paid off," he commented. "Later."

Street watched them go, and heard the companion say, "You should've let me kick his ass."

And Gamble responded, "I just saved *your* ass."

Sanchez came closer, but she too was still watching the two unhappy men retreat.

"What was that all about? Ex-cop?"

"Yeah." Street sighed. "He's an ex-cop, all right."

"But this was personal, I take it."

"Yeah . . . guess it's obvious."

"You gonna tell me? Or should I just ask around?"

Clearly she had picked up on the hidden facts. This was personal, but also had to do with police business, his career, his past, and she probably had also figured it had to do with why he had been kicked off S.W.A.T. and his being so eager to get back on. Didn't take a genius, and Sanchez was clever enough to connect these kinds of dots.

He could protest all he wanted. She'd blow his cover if she just asked around a little. No point hiding.

"He was my partner. We got in trouble. We acted on our own to save the life of a hostage. We went outside the box and used our judgment. It worked that time, but could just as easily have gone sour. I don't know . . . just the call of whoever's looking, I guess. He walked out. I stayed and ate shit for six months."

He walked her out to the marina, where dozens upon dozens of yachts lay in repose, pricking the night sky with gleaming aluminum masts, reflecting the black water on their white hulls, and catching the street lamps on royal blue or forest green sail covers, each speaking of a life so far out of Street's financial range that he couldn't even afford the docking fees. Still, he liked to look at them and dream.

Sanchez led the way to her car, as if she needed to be escorted. Wouldn't it be a riot to have some drunken chump try to put moves on an off-duty S.W.A.T. cop?

Suddenly he didn't feel like being alone.

"How long have you got the baby-sitter for?" he asked.

She rolled her eyes. "Just 'cause I bought you one drink doesn't mean you're getting laid."

There was an insult in there somewhere, though he wasn't sure which one of them should be insulted. He thought about pointing out that maybe he just wanted company and maybe he didn't have in mind what she thought he did.

What was the point? She wouldn't believe him.

"What does two drinks mean?" he muttered. This was getting annoying. She just automatically assumed everybody had it in for a woman who could take care of herself.

She paused, seemed to sense his disappointment and his lack of sexual threat to her.

"How'd you like to come over to my house?" she asked.

Though surprised, he simply admitted, "Your place, my place—mistake either way."

She shook her head. "Tomorrow. My kid's birthday party. How'd you like to come?"

"Tomorrow?"

"Why don't you come over?"

"I'm . . . hosting a Tupperware party."

"Tupperware."

"Really seals in the freshness. Party's completely booked. Otherwise, I'd invite you."

Now who was bullshitting whom, exactly?

Sanchez quirked her lips and said, "So I'll see you tomorrow? Round noon?"

She didn't wait for an answer this time, since the first one had been so ditzy. She got in her car without another glance, insisting by her manner that he just shut the devil up and do what she said to do, listen to somebody else for a change. Get his mind off things.

Therefore, he did. Never let it be said that James Street couldn't take an order or know one when he heard it. At least, never let it be said *anymore*.

*　　*　　*

He arrived at her house, a nice little Cape Cod place nestled in a neighborhood that was inexpensive but clean, generally safe, and nested in one of the older areas of Los Angeles, mostly homes built as workers' homes for the burgeoning film industry in the 1930s.

He brought the little girl a book. He didn't even know for sure what age connected with which type of book, but he got one on dinosaurs and figured it was a good bet for most kids these days.

Christine Sanchez was genuinely happy to see him, perhaps even genuinely surprised.

"Thanks for coming," she said.

"I got her a book," he began sheepishly, and handed over the package he had asked his neighbor lady to wrap. "I don't know if—"

"No, it's good," Sanchez cut off. "She reads. Come on in. You wanna cut the cake?"

"Whoa, the singular honor of the day? Sure, I do. Want me to use my duty knife?"

"Oh, yeah, let's do that. My daughter needs to see her cake hacked up in an assault maneuver."

"I could put the whole thing on the ceiling."

"I know you could! No, no, this way. That's the garage. We're on the patio."

Within five minutes a kid's birthday party was transformed to a scene of supreme violence. Screaming, shooting, falling, dying.

"No!" Street called, covered his face, and fell to the ground. The assailants showed him no mercy, firing wildly and howling with joy. After all, what could you do in a Super Soaker fight except fight back and die on command?

Street rolled in the grass as ten kids assaulted him viciously, the way they'd learned to in all their video games. The bad guy was down and out, which of course meant keep shooting until you were out of water.

He was rolling around between kids, making sure they each got a good shot at him, when he heard Beethoven's Fifth playing against his belt.

His beeper!

He sat up, dripping, in time to see Sanchez checking her own beeper.

Could it be? The very next day after the final?

Could it be *today*?

Deke rolled around the grocery store with a shopping cart, as he did every Saturday morning, this time with all three of his kids. At eight, eleven, and thirteen, they were almost as much help as they were hindrance, although his shopping list seemed to be about four times longer when they were with him than when they weren't. All of a sudden he was obliged to pick up candied fruit rolls, instant lemonade, fresh raspberries, frozen pizza rolls, chocolate peanut butter, and about two dozen other things that would never occur to him if he were shopping alone or with his wife.

And they were all arms! Things ended up in the cart that he never even saw go in there. He was shopping with a giant octopus! Snatch! Grab! Lick!

"Hey—who put these bottled iced teas in there?" he wailed as they clattered up to the checkout. "And what's with the individually wrapped nutty clusters? Do you know how much those cost for the weight of the package? I gotta teach you animals to shop efficiently!"

"This is health food, man," his eldest protested, shaking a can of Pringles.

"On your planet or mine, *man*?"

They laughed at him and he started reading off the ingredients of the Pringles, when his pager went off.

S.W.A.T.!

"Wow, Dad—this is it!" his youngest said, and the middle kid started clapping.

The cashier, a friendly eccentric named Cleo, said, "It's okay. I'll ring it up and have it sent over!"

"Thanks! Come on, kids!" Deke led the race outside. "It's time to ruin Mommy's day off!"

The first hole, and all morning to go.

Why did people always golf so early? Because it was pretty and solemn, cool and twinkly.

Anyway, that was Hondo's reason and his analysis.

He lined up a putt as Velasquez watched, enjoying a cigar.

When Hondo made the putt, the lieutenant complained, "How'd I ever let you con me into playing for money?"

Then both their pagers went off at the same

time. Quite a coincidence, although probably not unheard of . . . unless . . .

They checked, and looked at each other.

Yes!

Boxer sat on his couch, watching Jerry Springer talking to a transvestite who thought his/her legal domestic rights extended to his/her pet orangutan if they got married. That wasn't even the weirdest part. He/she had the monkey dressed as a—

"I thought you said you'd fix the sink!"

His wife. He *had* promised. On the weekend, he'd said, for the past four weekends. Instead, he'd usually spent the weekends pumping iron or running or involving himself in his favorite sport: talk and reality shows.

Most of these shows, he was damned sure, were scripted somehow. It's not like there couldn't be people this bizarre, with seriously demented attitudes and a desire to show all their dirty laundry in public, but he'd toyed around with being a guest on one of these shows as more or less an undercover study and been told that if he failed to appear, one of the in-house producers or standbys would just take his part and play it to the hilt. It was ad-lib central, and anything was okay as long as there was eventually a fight on stage.

Still, there was something about the transvestite and the monkey that just seemed like it was probably all true.

What'd the guy just say? An orangutan isn't a monkey? It's an ape?

Who cares?

"This is educational television, honey!" he called. "You ought to come out here and watch with me! This dweeb wants to marry his monk—his ape!"

Boxer knew perfectly well he wouldn't be able to use the orangutan as much of an anti-plumbing excuse, but when his pager went off, he not only had a surge of excitement for the first S.W.A.T. activity, but also for a legitimate out!

"Call a plumber!" he shouted. "I gotta go!"

"You said you'd fix it. You call a plumber."

"I just got the call!"

"You're always getting the call—"

But the door slammed behind him before he could even ask her what the heck she meant by that. He was S.W.A.T. and somebody needed him. This was his first chance. Reality calling— *real* reality.

"So how long have you been . . . dancing?"

"Stripping, you mean. It's okay, T.J., I like the job. I've been doing this about three years. Putting myself through technical school too. I would never be able to make this kind of money, y'know, answering phones or cleaning houses, y'know, or working in a flower shop or a deli. All the deli jobs are took up by all the unemployed actresses."

"Right. I get what you mean. Can I top off your drink?"

Monique smiled at T.J. in a seductive way, though he knew she was basically just a professional at that smile.

"A police officer who drinks Dom Perignon," she commented. "You're a real . . ."

"Mystery?"

"Hoot!"

"I may work in the mud," he said, handling the bottle gently, "but I like to play in the clouds."

She blushed, and this time seemed sincere. A stripper seduced. Mission accomplished, Officer.

"That's really romantic," she told him.

He grinned. "Yeah, I came up with it on my own."

His glass moved closer to hers. The clink of destiny—he listened for it, waited to feel the *ting* of the glass rims on each other, solidifying an evening well planned and pleasantly executed for a single cop and a particularly skilled exotic entertainer putting herself through technical school. Something about that last part was interesting and made her a higher charm in his mind, as if she had a goal beyond her station. He liked that. He understood her.

She wanted better in life, not just more money. She made plenty good money, he knew, right where she was, in a well—managed club with restrictions that protected the girls. She could stay there for years and have a good income. She was young enough, firm enough, had legs all the way to the ground, and an angelic twinkle in her eye that pretended just the right amount of innocent tease. Yet, she wanted more. Not just more money, but more out of life.

T.J. was the same. He could stay a street cop, maybe move up to the detective bureau eventually, go to the crime lab or forensics, even eventually command, and that was where he would go willingly, had fate not intervened in the form of Hondo.

Now he would be S.W.A.T., an officer who handled rare and heightened danger, whose career could hang on a split decision, and hair's breadth choices.

He wasn't worried about the danger. He was worried about finding himself in the kind of situation that had compromised Jim Street and torn apart a working unit in just seconds, because of unpredictability and elastic judgment calls. Before, when he wasn't on S.W.A.T., it was easy to make decisions after the barn doors slammed shut.

Now, though, he knew he might find himself in the same situation, having to make a choice when the answers were unclear and the lines blurred, even choosing between certain people to live and others to die. He wouldn't be just cleanup crew anymore when it came to law enforcement. He would be there to dirty things up, to add complication, and to bring an end to situations with no clear endings.

All at once he was part of a bizarre angle of law enforcement, where he had to think and sometimes even act like a criminal, with an enhanced possibility of having to kill for the purpose of saving lives. Every cop faced that willingly, but to be S.W.A.T—

His pager went off and nearly caused heart failure. He checked it, then closed his eyes for a moment to gather his nerves back into one bundle.

"I have to go!"

Monique's eyes flickered with congratulations at his first S.W.A.T. maneuver. "That's okay! I'll have lunch and you call me when you're done! I'll meet you at your cloud!"

"Sounds good!"

He took out his wallet, dumped five twenties on the table, and tried to extricate himself from the flowing tablecloth.

"Don't forget," she said quickly, "we ordered the Dom!"

T.J. smiled, and dumped another hundred on the table before dashing for the door.

11

AH, LUNCH. DEPUTY NILS KLEPKE RETURNED TO HIS DESK with a promising bundle packed by his wife into an insulating vinyl lunch tote. Chicken salad sandwich, made with rotisserie chicken, celery, carrots, celery salt, a big deli bun, and shredded lettuce. Applesauce with cinnamon for dessert, and chocolate milk. Nirvana on Earth. What an intelligent guy he was to marry Nancy when he had the chance.

He was used to processing endless drab information. His duty was an unending Rolodex of mug shots, arrest records, official letters, subpoenas, transfer orders, news articles, warrants, updates, court papers, and on and on, each a leaf on a very big and important tree. He had the ultimate "somebody's gotta do it" job, and indeed, somebody really did have to.

He knew, if no one else did, that if his little cog ever stopped turning, the whole law enforcement community would get constipation. No, this job wasn't fancy or elegant, had little promise for fame or even much advancement, but he liked doing it and he knew it was important. He knew the people who made the world turn were just as important as those who got the big bucks for big movements. Secretaries were critical to the business world, and cashiers were critical to the retail market, no matter how unglamorous their jobs might be. So were the clerks in the field of law enforcement, the people working in the underpinning halls of justice who didn't end up on TV. From the guys down in the crime lab to the gals who answered the phones in the prosecutors' offices, what if they suddenly weren't there? Or just started doing their jobs badly?

Wouldn't it be great to have Hollywood do a cop show about a law enforcement clerk? Imagine all the little stories and scaffolds that would seem to crumble if he pulled all his dozens of plugs . . . hmmm . . . maybe he'd write some of his stories down, just to see if anybody nipped. Just like fishing.

He almost had his sandwich built—Nancy always packed the individual items separately so the bread wouldn't get soggy—when he glanced at his computer screen, then looked a second time and almost crapped his trousers.

The lettuce went on the floor. The bun fell onto his keyboard, along with half the chicken salad.

Interpol!

His printer coughed out a photograph.

Klepke dumped his lunch all over his desk, raked the photograph out of the printer, then the accompanying warrant just as it sizzled out of the slot.

And he started running.

The department's main-level hallway had never seemed this long before. . . .

Within ten minutes he found himself the center of attention for more than his allotted fifteen minutes. A circus exploded around him and kept swirling for the rest of the day, a day he would tell his grandchildren about someday.

He thought of his two little kids, four and six years old, a girl and a boy, and imagined them out on the mean streets with this character in charge. Someday he would tell his kids about the small part he played in putting this man away, in crippling the criminal empire this man had spun, and how this terrible person had once been just a child in a backyard who had made certain choices and with those selections destroyed many lives.

While doing the unusual work of the hour, he rehearsed the speech in his head, even though actually speaking it would be years away. He would wait until they were old enough to have some idea of the kind of crimes he was referring to, and it would probably happen on the same day as the "don't smoke, don't steal, and don't drive drunk" speech.

But why, Daddy? Everybody does it.

The sheriff, the under-sheriff, all the lieutenants,

several sergeants, and mayor's office brass after brass flooded into his cubicle, clogging up his concentration until he had to fight for stability. He got clapped on the back more times in one hour than he had in his whole life. They told him what a miracle he performed and how simple clerks could make the world go around if they did their jobs with conscience and alertness. They talked about how easily this fax could've slipped through his fingers or ended up in the wastebasket if not for him.

Somebody even called him "Eagle-eye" and talked about a promotion.

He enjoyed all this, basking in the light of attention that his job, his personality, and his talents would never otherwise merit. Enjoyed it a lot . . . until somebody else came in and said, "The Feds are here."

A mobile command unit had been set up on an otherwise quiet neighborhood street in Central L.A. The target was a house that was completely unkempt, unmowed, unattended in the middle of an otherwise pristine and manicured subdivision.

This house, the one they were here for, was in fact boarded up, and there was trash strewn about the excuse for a lawn. Judging by the length of the rough grass and its brown crunchy condition, this house hadn't been tended in at least two months, but other things spoke of even longer abandonment.

Street and Sanchez pulled up in Street's personal car. T.J., Boxer, and Deke were already here, already changing into their gear. As soon as everyone was here, Hondo hurried to them.

"The reason our much needed day of God-appointed rest was interrupted is that we have a Polish hostage."

"So what if he's Polish?" Deke asked.

"No, no," Hondo said. He formed his hand into a gun and held it to his head. "It means, If anyone comes in, I'm blowing my *own* head off. Negotiations aren't going anywhere. This guy is off his meds. T.J., grab your 308 and hit the high ground with Boxer. Sanchez, Deke, you got rear guard. Street, you got me."

They flinched as a shotgun shot *thwacked* from inside the house.

"I want a limo!"

"Who the hell is—" Deke blurted.

"It's him," Street mentioned, buckling his equipment on. "The guy inside."

"Oh."

"And a twelve-pack!"

"Heck, we ought to just give him those," Sanchez commented. "I thought my first S.W.A.T. assignment would be a little bigger than this."

"They're all big," Street said, "even the little ones."

She twisted her mouth in mock shame. "I guess you're right about that. Sorry."

"I saw your mother cross herself when we got the call. Doesn't she know all our duty isn't hazardous?"

"In her rational mind she knows it. Oh—wait. She doesn't have a rational mind. Guess she doesn't know it."

"I'll tell her, if you want. Mama, police work is eighty percent paperwork and waiting around. Don't let the nutcase with the shotgun blindly firing out his front door bother you any—"

"Here comes the lieutenant."

Street clammed up on cue and turned.

Lieutenant Velasquez hurried to them, already talking.

"We keep lobbing gas, this guy is still smoking cigarettes and popping off shotgun rounds through his front door."

Street nodded and managed not to say *no shit*.

"Let's go hard in the back with the shields," Hondo suggested, ready and willing to use his team to end the situation sooner than later.

Velasquez waggled his head in doubt. "He claims to have all the windows and doors wired and plastic explosives."

Hondo rolled his eyes. "Come on, Greg . . ."

"You wrote the book. I just read it. Let's hear some suggestions."

"I got one," Street began, and opened up the hatch of his SUV.

Inside was his little invention. The one he'd been perfecting during his time off the team. The others peered into the hatch. Hondo smiled.

Moments later, they were tying the "Key to the City" to an L.A.P.D. towing truck.

Hondo spoke into his radio. "We're ready."

Street motioned to Deke and Sanchez. "Go."

Deke broke running, with Street paralleling him, carrying the heavy contraption, and Sanchez covering. They ran to the side of the house, gaining speed. Street released the grapples, which spread its barbed wire like a giant fishhook.

KPOK!

The grapples shot from their housing and slammed into the side of the house, going right through the wall structure, then popping out to their full-dispersal range.

Through the hole they heard the Polish hostage saying, "It's the damn robot aliens!"

Street motioned Deke to stand clear, then yelled, "Hit it!" and signaled the tow truck driver. The big truck roared as its engine was gunned.

The cable grew taut in a single snapping motion, took instant tension, and twisted with effort. The house began to groan.

In a moment it was shrieking. Wood strained, lath cracked, rebar howled—and finally the entire side of the house was ripped outward as if sucked by a tornado.

The Polish hostage stood there in his underwear. Red underwear, with little speckles that looked like—yes, little white hearts.

All at once there were ten full-geared S.W.A.T. officers swarming the hole, each one yelling, "Down! Down on the ground! Drop the gun! Down on the ground!"

What pleasant music.

Hondo turned away, so no one could see him laughing.

But Street saw it, and he was proud.

"Damn, man," Deke commented, "you need to be selling this on eBay!"

"Only got one," Street said.

"I'll handle the marketing. Fifty-fifty! We'll both get rich. Give 'Key to the City' a whole new meaning!"

Sanchez came up, beginning to take off her gear as the nutcase was hauled away by other officers. "Well, I can now officially tell my mother that S.W.A.T. duty is safe, cute, fun, and not really very dangerous. Based on one encounter, that is."

"This was dangerous!" Street protested. "Look! I got a sliver!"

"We'll give you a Purple Heart," T.J. said as he joined them, with Boxer close behind.

"Is it always this easy?" Boxer asked. "I didn't even need to put my shoes on."

T.J. elbowed him. "Hey, it got you out of your plumbing, didn't it?"

"Yeah, sure did. You know anything about soil pipes?"

"Nothing. Not a thing. I swear. Never heard of it. Don't ask me again. I'm joining the Witness Protection Program."

"Be at my house at five-thirty!"

"Name's gonna be Guido. Guido Schroeder. Vat iss zoil pipe? I never hear zoil pipe. No speek Engleesh."

"I have you now, Luke Skywalker."

They were all laughing by the time Lieutenant Velasquez crossed to them from wherever he'd just been. He put his hand on Boxer's flak vest just as he was taking it off.

"Hold it. Sheriff's Department just called. We've been holding a high-priority international racketeer and didn't even know it!"

"Not surprising," Hondo drawled. "Need us for escort?"

"You're closest," the lieutenant said. "Get the prisoner to HQ."

"Will do. All right, people, suit back up. Street, drive the Suburban. The rest of you, bring your own cars along. This won't be nothin', either."

Boxer made a show of stomping his foot and wailed, "But I just found Guido's Superior Sanitation and Plumbing Service! I need to go home and continue being the ideal husband and house-maintenance hero!"

Street shook his head. "I think we know where the sanitation is needed."

T.J. followed as they struck off for the S.W.A.T. Suburban and their cars. "No speeka Engleesh, homies. Want Whopper with flies. You buy."

The sheriff's prisoner-transport bus had a low front tire. The driver could tell because the vehicle wanted to go right all the time, and he knew it had just been aligned. He only had an hour left on his watch and could hand it over to the next guy with orders to fill the tire. There were perks to seniority.

Oh, what now? There was an L.A.P.D. patrol car, all lit up and flashing, tailing the bus.

He picked up the radio.

"This is Nine-Tom-King transporting inmates to Superior. A black-and-white is signaling a pull-over."

"Ten-four," the dispatcher responded. *"Hold the line to confirm."*

His orders were not to pull over for any reason other than injury, and even then he was supposed to drive to a hospital where he could be met by backup officers. He had a busload of dangerous convicts here, and there was just him and the other deputy guard in the back to stand between peace and real trouble.

"Dispatch to Nine-Tom-King."

"Roger, go ahead."

"There's a problem with one of your transports. The unit signaling is probably providing interception. Can you read his patrol number?"

"Stand by . . . roger. One-one-zero-seven. That's one-one-zero seven."

"Hold while I confirm."

The deputy in the back came forward. "What's up?"

"That black-and-white's tailing us with his lights on. Wants us to pull over."

"So pull over."

"But it's not an authorized stop. Dispatch is

checking the reason. Says there's something going on with one of these prisoners."

"If there's something going on and Dispatch knows it, go ahead and pull over."

"Yeah . . . I guess so."

The bus slowly maneuvered to the left and snugged up to the curb.

The black-and-white pulled around them and stopped in front, positioning itself so that the bus couldn't possibly pull out. It was an odd maneuver for cops to do to other cops, but the driver chalked it up to just habit on the part of a road patrol officer. He probably pulled over thirty people a week and always pulled in front of their cars.

Each officer had a different preference, and some departments had policy.

But he didn't like not being able to pull away. It went against his grain. Anything that forestalled his duty to deliver these prisoners made him nervous.

His partner approached the bus door after making sure all the prisoners were secure and couldn't take advantage of the odd moment.

There was a big cop, swarthy and not very contented, in uniform, stepping out of the patrol car, moving toward them with a sort of determination in his face. He wore sunglasses. Wasn't even that bright out.

In the patrol car, behind the wheel, remained another cop, his sour face glaring at the prison bus driver. How could these two get in such a bad mood so early in the afternoon?

"I'll get the door," the deputy said.

"I guess," the driver responded, and shrugged. He eyed the Duress button.

The deputy leaned out the now-open door to greet the uniform. Not so much as a single word left his throat before it was blown open by the uniformed cop striding toward them.

The driver flinched, twisted in his seat, but only in time to see the deputy slump forward and then to be mystically shoved back into the bus, as if floating, to land on the floor in a heap. The loud bark of handgun fire ruined the quiet day, and the deputy was destroyed.

The driver tried to reach toward the Duress button. His finger went out before him in slow motion, nearly there, nearly there—

In the rearview mirror he caught the astonished eyes of the inmates in the prisoner cage as the slaughter continued. In a small fraction of a second, he noted that they all looked surprised except that one skinny guy, the one who hadn't made a bit of trouble and had even claimed that nobody had to worry about him. He would be calm and easy to transport. No problem, Officers. He just wanted to cooperate.

Now there was slaughter happening.

The deputy must be dead, with all those slugs slamming into his bulky body.

But no . . . this time it was the driver himself being slaughtered. He saw blood on his hand before it reached the button. He saw his hand begin to fall, the bus floor to tip, the steering wheel to come slanting toward his face. He felt the blow of the wheel on his forehead, a heavy and hollow *bonk*.

As he died, he slumped there with his eyes open, twisted in his seat almost halfway around, thinking about the unsurprised man in back.

Because now that man was smiling.

The man lifted his shackled arms. "Let's go! Get these off!" he ordered.

Amazingly, the uniformed cop who had just shot two fellow officers rifled the keys from the deputy and began to do as the prisoner ordered him to. Why would he do that?

In the distance, over a mountain and through a mist, the paralyzed driver heard the voice of Central Dispatch. His own lips moved, but no sound came out of them.

Dispatch was calling. Somebody . . . please answer her . . . please respond . . .

"Nine-Tom-King, there's a problem. Nine-Tom-King, do you copy? Nine-Tom-King, acknowledge."

12

"Nine-Tom-King, this is Thirty-David-Three. What's your twenty?"

All eyes searched for the bus as the S.W.A.T. Suburban, and the two cars tailing it scanned the cityscape for the vehicle everyone wanted to find. It should be responding. Why wasn't it?

Jim Street kept the Suburban at a steady but fairly high speed, lights going so the other traffic pulled over. They scanned for the prison bus. What was going on, anyway?

"On the right," he noticed. "There it is, on Wilcox."

"This is Thirty-David-Three," Hondo said immediately to Dispatch. "I have eyes on the bus. Wilcox and Hollywood."

Street craned a little as he maneuvered the Suburban toward the parked bus and turned onto Wilcox Boulevard. A uniformed officer was escorting a prisoner from the bus toward a black-and-white parked at an angle in front of the bus.

"Looks like the uniform's got it handled," he noted.

Hondo raised the mic. "Dispatch, we're all clear. A black-and-white is on the scene."

The cop with the prisoner waved an "everything's okay" gesture when he saw the Suburban closing in.

"Thirty-David-Three, Dispatch. We do not have a positive ID on that black-and-white. They're also not responding. Is there an officer in the unit?"

"Affirmative, Dispatch, I can see a driver. Why wouldn't he be answering—"

The uniformed officer with the prisoner approached the passenger side of the patrol car. He hurried a little as the Suburban approached.

Street's hands started to tingle on the steering wheel. The cop was hurrying too much, too anxiously. Something about his body language . . . Street slowed the Suburban to a stop about twenty feet earlier than he normally would, but before he could galvanize what he was sensing into anything he might act upon, the uniform shoved the prisoner into the backseat of the black-and-white, disappeared from the waist up for a second, and came out with an AK-47!

Nobody even got a *shit!* shouted before the bullets rattled across the grill of the Suburban and the uniform shifted his shoulder to improve his aim. His second burst of shots splattered across the windshield, but by then Street and Hondo were unflinchingly returning fire, also right through the windshield.

Like a timed ballet, Street knew to aim at the uniform while Hondo aimed at the fake cop behind the wheel. Hondo got his man, then ducked as the uniform fired again from a protected spot in front of the black-and-white unit.

Slugs slammed through the Suburban, slaughtering the seats, but Street hadn't waited. He threw the door open, tumbled out of the vehicle onto the pavement, already rolling when he hit the ground, and still firing all the way. He made a spectacle of himself, drawing fire away from Hondo and the other two cars with his partners inside. He strained his legs to put himself back on his feet and weaved wildly as the AK made its trademark *brrrrdttt* three more times before Street could pause, aim, and finally take a killing shot.

The fake uniformed officer was struck in the neck, his carotid artery and part of his jaw destroyed.

When the assailant went down, Boxer and T.J. jumped out of their car and approached the bus, weapons drawn. Only an instant later, Deke and Sanchez pulled up, just late enough to miss the hyperspeed action.

No, it wasn't over! The prisoner pushed the fake cop out the driver's door, and suddenly the black-and-white peeled out with an earsplitting scream.

Street opened fire again. So did Hondo and Boxer, lathering the escaping unit with bullets. But this was a police car and hard to stop. Street wanted to fire more, but suddenly the background was bad. Tourists and shoppers, residents and every other manner of civilian had appeared to have a look at whatever was happening. They were in the line of fire. Some noticed and quickly got down or backed off, but others were too stupid to overcome their curiosity with common sense.

Swearing under his breath, Street restrained himself and held his fire, but struck off running at full speed, crossing the other S.W.A.T officers' lines of fire without even thinking about the risk to himself.

Just as the squad car howled into a slalom down the street, Sanchez accelerated her car in a straight line right at the escaping black-and-white. Because the black-and-white had to veer twice to avoid parked vehicles, the distance closed almost instantly. Sanchez had guts—she never applied the brakes. She sped right toward the squad car and T-boned it at only the slightest angle as it tried to twist onto the straightaway of Hollywood Boulevard.

The loud bang resounded down the open boulevard.

Street kept running. He'd seen plenty of vehicles take hits like that and keep going. This one, though, was disabled well enough that one of the tire wells was destroyed and kept the wheel from turning, though the driver was trying to pull away.

In his mind Street began to gel the circumstances. He'd almost held back firing at men in police uniforms because his mind just didn't work like that. Until the bullets actually struck his windshield, he hadn't been able to add up that these cops were fake and what he was seeing wasn't a prisoner transfer—it was an escape attempt that damned near succeeded given a few more critical seconds. From here they could've gone in any of ten directions and vanished into the great sprawling city.

He dodged around a tree, and by the time he got to the other side of the tree, everything had changed again. The prisoner was out of the car and running!

Street, at full clip, twisted on the inside of one foot and changed his direction to follow.

There were people everywhere. He couldn't open fire. The prisoner ran like a rabbit a half block in front of him, but Street was closing. He sucked three quick lung-fillers and poured on the speed, elbows pumping.

The guy threw a quick glance over his shoulder and saw Street tightening the distance between them. Somehow, without really stopping, the guy twisted around—was he giving up?

No, he had a gun!

He was training it on Street when the distance finally closed. The prisoner got off one wild shot that whizzed past Street's right shoulder, and then he was on top of the creep.

They both went down hard on the sidewalk outside of the famous Mann's Chinese Theatre, sprawling all over the signatures and footprints of

Hollywood stars. Street found his balance and got a knee into the guy's back, but the wiry prisoner wasn't giving up yet, and twisted under Street's weight until he was almost free again. He snatched up a piece of broken glass and in a single swipe slashed at Street's head.

Street caught the movement in the corner of his eye and managed to veer just enough to his right that the assault missed his artery and just got the left earlobe.

Using all his strength, Street slammed his pistol into the guy's wrist, disabling him. The glass went skittering under a parked car. He put his foot on the prisoner's spine and pulled the guy up by one arm until a squawk of pain came as a reward. Then the cuffs came out and it was all over.

By the time he had both wrists cuffed behind this joker's back, the rest of the team skidded to a stop around them.

"You all right?" Hondo asked quickly.

Street started to respond, but his friend on the ground twisted again, revealing the Hollywood star of Alex Trebek.

"Ten more seconds," the guy swore, "and you would've been dead."

"Yeah, I've been dead a lot of times," Street snarled back. "Son of a bitch, who the hell are you? Then again, who the hell cares?"

"I got him, Jim," Boxer said as he and Deke snagged the virulent criminal and pulled him away from Street.

Street paused, bleeding, and blinked at the abrupt intimacy offered from unlikely quarters.

"Good thing you could run him down," Hondo told him, glancing around at the rubberneckers. "We couldn't get a single clean shot once he started hoofin'."

"You okay?" T.J. offered him a gauze pad from his first-aid pocket.

"I don't know," Street said. "Can't see it. How's it look?"

"Just cut the lobe and scored the side of your neck a little bit."

"Then I guess I'm okay." He turned to the bad guy, whose gaunt cheeks and ethnic eyes created an air of the mysterious and exotic, but the dangerous kind. The man's eyes were layered with experience and threat. "Who in blazes is this guy?"

"It was an explosive and deadly day in Hollywood as a gun battle erupted between armed suspects and members of the L.A.P.D.'s elite S.W.A.T. Unit. Details are still sketchy but sources tell us there were fatalities, including two L.A. County Sheriffs. Stay tuned as more details on this bloody encounter come to us here at your in-touch news source . . ."

LOS ANGELES CITY HALL

The steps were packed with reporters and minicams as the news media raucously set up their equipment for a press conference, each wanting the scoop on a very dramatic day in Hollywood.

And it wasn't over. Street was given the honor of escorting the cocky skinny inmate he'd collared up the steps so the world could get a good gander at this creep and his odds of ever going incognito again would be greatly diminished. Hondo and the other team members provided very close backup, but let Street lead the way toward the podium where the deputy police chief was stepping up for the press conference.

The deputy chief gave them a nod of approval and began immediately to address the clutch of reporters.

"Okay, please—we're ready here. Ladies and gentlemen, please!"

It took a couple of seconds for the reporters to settle down, but finally they did.

"It was a big day," the deputy chief went on. "Captain Tom Fuller from S.W.A.T. is going to brief you on this afternoon's events. Afterward, I'll take your questions."

Fuller stepped up to the podium, a bit flushed at having to report the excellent work of these people whom he had so heartily resisted only a matter of hours before. But he liked the stage, enjoyed talking to the public, and in just a few moments that took over and he was right at home.

"At one forty-five P.M., a Sheriff's Department bus was assaulted by two suspects with AK-47s in an attempted breakout of a jail inmate. All of law enforcement deeply regrets the loss of two deputy sheriffs. One of the S.W.A.T. units I command engaged the gunmen on scene, after which the two suspects were fatally shot. S.W.A.T. then prevented the escape of the inmate, Alexander Lupin, a French national who has now been positively identified as 'Le Loup Rouge.' "

He paused on cue, knowing this would take a couple of rounds to sink in.

"A what rouge?" a reporter blurted.

Street was glad somebody else asked, because he had no idea what that meant.

Fuller spoke louder, a little more clearly. "Le . . . Loup . . . Rouge. It's French for 'the Red Wolf.' He's wanted by Interpol and more than ten national governments, including our own, on charges of arms dealing, drug trafficking, extortion, smuggling, kidnapping, and over two dozen murders—"

He paused again as the crowd rustled with astounded appreciation for this roster of life accomplishments.

"—murders he's either ordered to be committed, or committed himself," the captain continued. He slowed down a little, probably not wanting to have to repeat himself.

The reporters shifted again somewhat, but no one made a sound. Cameras whirred and a few flashes went off, catching Street, the other S.W.A.T. members, and Alexander Lupin and his damned attitude. This guy was a real cracker. He actually liked the attention and the reading off of his accomplishments. He even smiled once—a real smile, not just one of those nervous ones.

"For the last two years," Fuller continued evenly, "he's been untraceable, unarrestable, to the point many in the law enforcement questioned whether he was even still alive. Today we can safely say the Red Wolf is alive . . . and in custody."

If this had been a regular audience, there would've been applause. Street could feel the inclination running through the reporters, even to the point where they glanced at each other to see if anybody else was going to start the round.

Nobody did, though everyone felt the stirring of pride and success, and he and the other S.W.A.T. officers enjoyed several congratulatory smiles and the impressed gazes of the hard-bitten reporters who thought they'd heard just about everything this dirty world could offer up.

They weren't looking at your average crime boss here. This was an international racketeer, a man who could pull strings across continents. What had been crippled today was a criminal network probably going back generations, and which would've gone forward even more generations if not brought to the skids here and now.

Oh, somebody would filter to the top to take this chief's place, but it would take years to rebuild a structure like Alexander Lupin's, the brand of stacked debts, loyalties, threats, warnings, obligations, devotions, and thousands of other carefully built structural pieces that made up a strong crime network. While the Lupin syndicate might not go away completely, it would be severely diminished, probably for a decade or more. They were holding in their hands many other lives—murders which would never now take place, drugs which would never be funneled into the country, extortion which would never be taken seriously, and probably an upheaval in command authority which would ripple worldwide and crumble many carefully stacked towers.

Jim Street was—admit it—proud of himself. He hadn't done anything particularly special or hard, but he had done it right and in the right order. He hadn't opened fire just because he had a clean shot. Nobody could say he endangered lives this time. Was he growing a discretion bone or what?

And at the same moment he had to wonder if his hesitation had really been fear. Not for his life but for his career. He hadn't wanted to be kicked off S.W.A.T after one day. Why had he hesitated? Why, really?

Today it had worked. What if it didn't work the next time?

Here they were, on display for the media hounds, and no matter how magnetic the cameras were, Street discovered he was nervous. Something about this Lupin guy stirred up the wrong kind of attention, the kind of notoriety given to the Capones and Gottis, not the famous but the infamous. He scanned the herd and focused in on the nearest reporter, standing like a mannequin before a cameraman.

"This is Alex Lupin," the reporter explained in that

media voice we all recognize. "He's an international fugitive wanted in over a dozen countries. The State Department is calling his arrest 'historic.' Domestic and foreign law-enforcement agencies are already jockeying to interrogate the man one high-level White House aide dubbed simply 'The Catch.' "

"Let's get him to solitary," Hondo murmured. He'd had about enough of press coverage and didn't want to take any more chances. They'd had their look at the animal in question.

"Right," Street responded. "This way, Prince Charming."

He began to turn Lupin away from the clog of humanity.

Unexpectedly Alex Lupin began to go with him, then abruptly cranked around and faced the cameras and began to shout.

"I will give one hundred million dollars to whoever can break me out of jail!"

Surprised, Street blinked, then slammed his weapon into Lupin's kidneys and gave him a push. Hondo took the guy's arm and started pulling, but Lupin shouted again, louder.

"One hundred million dollars!"

The S.W.A.T. team swarmed Lupin and crushed him toward the door to the secured hallway.

As the doors slammed behind them, cutting them off from the ecstatic reporters with the phenomenal news story, Jim Street saw a twinkle and a twisted grin on Alex Lupin's face that caused his stomach to pinch.

With each step they took, the significance of what had just happened sank a little deeper in, and the voice kept echoing over and over, the sound of a giant sweet carrot being dangled before the eyes of the planet's greedy underworld.

"One hundred million . . . One hundred million . . . One hundred million dollars . . ."

Everyone, by five o'clock that night, had heard the wild promise made by the phenomenally wealthy crime boss. Speculative brains began stirring and simmering the numbers, the situation, the man himself, some serious, some not, many now locked in imagination of just how much money had been waved in front of their noses, and the noses of the unscrupulous of the world, from the gangster crash pads to the upscale lawyer bars, to the county jail to the biker hangouts.

"Hundred million sounds good to me."
"Hell, yeah!"
"Where's my gun?"

"Even if you just spin off the hundred mil into low-rate tax-free muni bonds, you're still clearing three or four million a year. Tax-free."
"Winters in Aspen, summers in Jamaica, a new chick every day . . ."
"Deep. Real deep."
"Exactly."

"You for real, man?"

Various prisoners pressed up against their cell bars as the S.W.A.T. team led Alex Lupin to his humble sleeping quarters, temporary though those would be. The Latino thug who had called out to Lupin grinned as he got a nod in response from the legendary criminal.

"A hundred million!" Lupin called back. "Tell your friends!"

"Keep moving," Deke ordered.

But they were all worried. Jails leaked like cheesecloth.

"Can you imagine that, folks? Can you imagine the balls on this guy? Thinking money can buy him out of jail? Who does he think he is? O.J.? Stay tuned for more on this story, right here on your favorite drive-time radio big blast in the big west! After this break for that down-and-dirty voyage into the great chasm of advertising bewonderment— our spectacular sponsors, who, by the way, have not offered us a hundred million dollars to keep you listening! Keep your hands off that dial!"

And in the depths of the desert, in a dilapidated ranch house surrounded by parked motorcycles, a pair of hands paused in their attempt to fit together the parts of a Yamaha two-stroke that had seen better days. The hands belonged to a man on the edge of life, a man who had once been clean-cut and better fed. He was a ghost of the icon he had once been. Over the past two days he hadn't even shaved, which had until now been his one daily practice that held him to his life before, the life as a soldier and police officer. Today he was as low as he ever had been, sitting at the bottom of a slide that had begun two nights ago in the beach pub while playing pool.

In the background two of his companions—he couldn't really say friends—were still playing pool on his table, avoiding the ripped part of the felt, which they'd tried to glue down last month, but which was now curling on the edges.

They paused in their game, wondering why he had suddenly stopped fixing the bike and had apparently lost interest in doing so. They were just looking at him. He saw them in his periphery, but they didn't interest him any more than the motorcycle did.

Something quite else had taken over his mind. Plans had begun to whirr inside his head. He didn't want them, necessarily, but they were there anyway. He was letting them develop, like a mental exercise. He just sat there on the unprotected floor, with a puddle of oil soaking into the hem of his jeans and the side of his sock.

What they thought, he didn't care. His time for caring what the world thought of him was long faded to dust.

He just sat, with Vise-Grips dangling from his

hand, and stared at the radio as it drummed a series of commercials.

The commercials, though, didn't interest him either. There was something else.

"We've been looking for this prick for a long time. A broken taillight took him down? Unbelievable!"

Hondo listened to the FBI agent—the guy's name was Hauser—but made no comment. He was the attending S.W.A.T. team member from the arresting squad. There were others here who were better to do the chitchatting.

Five other S.W.A.T. sergeants sat at the table in the Parker Center's Situation Room, along with Captain Fuller, Lieutenant Velasquez, Agent Hauser, and a second FBI special agent named Kirkland.

"The mayor and the chief," Fuller said after the amazement was handled, "want him handed over as soon as possible."

Agent Kirkland nodded. "The plan is to have you escort him to Twenty-Nine Palms, the Marine base out in the desert. He'll be nice and secure with a battalion of Marines guarding him."

"You might want to have some press photographers meet us at the base," Fuller added, "when my boys bring him in. It's a huge story."

And that was about as subtle as thunder. *When my boys bring him in.*

Hondo held his breath. Was Fuller actually enjoying the existence of the new S.W.A.T. unit for a change? Might he actually be . . . proud?

Agent Kirkland shrugged. "We'll pass that request up the ladder to D.C."

He and Hauser then got up and left.

Captain Fuller gave Hondo one of those looks you don't expect, and said, "If the papers spell my name right, it just might be your lucky day."

A few minutes later Hondo and the other S.W.A.T. sergeants were following Velasquez through the Parker Center corridors.

"An L.A.P.D. helicopter will arrive here at 1300," Velasquez was saying, "and transport the defendant. Until we get him inside the Marine brig, he's our baby. Sergeant Howard, your people have sniper detail. Sergeant Hondo, your team is escorting the prisoner. Sergeant Yamato, you guys back him up."

Everybody was glad for each detail. They were anxious, though they didn't say it out loud, to ditch this hot potato before any wiseass out there got some bright idea to get rich fast by breaking this smoldering ember out of their hands. Underneath the general belief that it couldn't be done with so much attention and firepower focused on keeping the guy in custody, Hondo knew that every officer on the force was concerned, and rightfully so.

Even if Lupin couldn't be wrenched away from the police, certainly the potential existed for some kind of disaster in any attempts that might be made.

And with that kind of money on the table, some mighty heavy hitters could be tempted to design and fund a pretty elaborate plan. Certainly Lupin's own crime organization would be mobilizing, whether any free agents did or not. Something would happen.

They had to move before it did. Urgency showed in the spring of every step, and declared itself in their grim silence.

There was a hallway near the helipad. The Parker Center had its own special entry systems and helicopter landing area on the roof. This move could be done with security. Hondo kept telling himself that, but the sense of having to move faster and faster just wouldn't go away.

He and his team led Alexander Lupin and his snide attitude through the Parker Center from the holding cells. Nobody wanted to touch him, but they had to. They were all business, no chitchat, and they all flinched when Hondo's radio cracked their wordless rush to the roof.

"This is Ten-David. Snipers have secured the perimeter."

Hondo responded. "Roger, Ten-David, we're coming out." To his team, he added, "Only got one chance to do it right."

They passed a couple of well-armed guards and were buzzed through to the outer door of the helipad.

Outside there was a sharp crosswind from the west, with a bit of the bitter Alaskan chill that constantly roared down from the north Pacific. Usually the chill didn't descend so close to the ground this time of year, but here it was. The people on the street level probably couldn't feel it at all.

Jim Street squinted into the bright sunlight at the vacant helipad. The chopper was on its way, scheduled not to arrive until the last minute. They were in contact.

He couldn't quite work up a damn about this piker Lupin. To look at him, he was just a nothing, a stunningly average foreigner with no sign of what must be a substantial intellect to run a huge crime organization. Or perhaps he was just ruthless enough and just well enough trained by those who had come before. Sometimes that combination would do. Any dynasty could be kept going with the right information passed along, and the right infrastructure inherited.

He wasn't ready to be impressed by this guy yet. His super crime network couldn't get to him up here, surrounded by S.W.A.T. officers, bristling with a hedge of snipers in position, scanning the city for incoming trouble. Nobody would throw a bomb, after all. Killing Lupin wouldn't get anybody anything.

"What's a hundred million split six ways?" Deke asked, eyeing Lupin with the same attitude Street had.

"Sixteen something," Boxer supplied.

"I could put the kids through college and still get a courtside Lakers seat right next to Jack. You, Sanchez?"

She scanned the roof from inside her helmet. "New house for my girl. Fenced-in backyard with a pool."

"Typical chick response," T.J. downplayed.

Sanchez ignored him and asked Boxer, "What would you buy?"

"My own town," Boxer said decisively, with his chin out. "Name it after myself."

Deke grimaced. "Boxerville?"

Sanchez smiled and looked at Street. "What would you do with the cash?"

Street pretended to think for a few seconds, as if scanning all his favorite catalogs in his mind's eye. "I'd buy Boxerville and change the name to Streetville."

Even Boxer smiled at that one.

So Street was right—the feud was starting to melt. He'd been afraid it was only his imagination and that one slip where Boxer actually called him by his first name. Maybe it wasn't a mistake or an illusion after all. It had been a long time since this many things had gone right for him in a row.

He hoped today wouldn't be the tiebreaker after such a great week. Things could go wrong. He wasn't so cocky that he didn't know that. With his own training he could think of several ways to get at Lupin. That meant somebody else could think of ways too.

"Why talk about it when you can have it?"

That was Alexander Lupin. His voice surprised them all. He hadn't said a word until now.

"Shut up," Hondo warned. "Let's be alert, team. We've got work to do. Here comes the chopper."

An L.A.P.D. Agusta-109 service helicopter approached the helipad a little faster than was really safe. Either the pilot was a hotshot or he wanted to get this show on the road.

Jim Street bet on a little of both. News of Alex Lupin's bold public declaration, a criminal call to action like no other, was spreading at hyperspeed. Fox News, MSNBC, and every other talk-heavy Klaxon station from radio to the Internet was already bubbling, replaying the amazing moment over and over, a moment when a master criminal freely used the world's media like a toy, to foment crime, to thwart justice, and with clear intent to kill anyone who got in his way.

This was not a call to action for decent people. Rather it was a mobilization of the most rapacious and conscienceless elements a complex society could possibly offer, and it stretched across all civilization within mere minutes. Even if they had no one more to deal with than Alex Lupin's personal loyalists, the threat of action had to be taken very seriously.

And Street knew the fan spread much wider than just Lupin's own circle. This master asshole suddenly had many more friends than his stained fingers could ever reach before. Before today Lupin benefited from being unknown to the general public. Today, though, he had learned the trick of wide-

ranging notoriety. He had seized the moment auda-
ciously, and they all knew the wild bet just might
pay off for Lupin if they weren't very careful. His
payoff meant the deaths of cops.

Don't let it happen. Don't let it happen.

He could too easily imagine how he would do
this. Long-range sniper shot . . . could set up any of
a dozen places, farther away than most people
would believe. There was no way to completely
protect this area. He glanced around at the distant
buildings that suddenly didn't seem so distant.
There were a dozen angles from which a shot could
strike something here on this helipad.

On it. Or above it.

The thought struck him like a hand across the
face. The chopper!

He crouched a little, knees bent, suddenly aware
not of himself, his partners, or even Alex Lupin,
but of the helicopter now maneuvering against the
crosswind, pivoting in a hover position over the helipad, moving forward only slightly as the pilot got
into a situation he liked for landing. Only three or
four more seconds went by.

The helicopter abruptly tilted sideways as if
dancing. Graceful, but ugly somehow. Its rotor hub
was splintering! The transmission housing—a perfect target. Hydraulic fluid sprayed like spit all over
the helipad and the chopper itself.

"They're hit!" Street shouted.

13

"WHAT'D YOU SAY?" T.J. ASKED.

Street gulped a breath. In the time it took him to do that a muffled *paaoooom* sounded over the landscape. Aftershock! The sound had taken a full second and more to reach them. He tried to calculate in his head what that meant, the distance, the trajectory—and he swung to look in the direction of the three—no, four—buildings that might fit the description of the numbers in his head.

"Some kind of massive-caliber explosive-tipped charge," Street called over the grumble of the wounded helicopter. "Probably .50! A bullet the size of a Magic Marker. Takes a scope the size of a man's arm to make that shot!"

He wasn't showing off. He really thought he might be the only one of them besides maybe Hondo who had ever heard a shot like that actually fired from a distance. He'd fired them and heard them fired while in the SEALs. Never thought he'd need to recall that sound!

The S.W.A.T. team all reacted as if a single animal, crouching and dragging Lupin down with them as the helicopter lost control and spun faster overhead, the pilot obviously struggling wildly for control and actually getting some.

"We're taking fire!" the radio crackled from the chopper. Losing hydraulic pressure fast!"

"Ten-David, come in," Hondo shouted into his microphone.

"Shots fired! Shots fired!" Lieutenant Velasquez's voice responded. "Anyone see where it came from?"

"Negative," one of the S.W.A.T. snipers answered. "No location on the shooter."

Street called over the grinding noise of the helicopter's damaged rotor. "I'd put it at one of those buildings!" He pointed to three of the four, having eliminated one because of angle and a tree in the line of fire.

Paaooooom oom oom

A second shot!

He looked—they all did—at the chopper. Sure enough, it was already hit before they heard the sound. The gearbox detonated with a terrible second explosion and a horrid grinding noise that pierced the daylight air and made them all crouch and squint with empathy and dread for the men inside.

CRACK

The rotor separated from the helicopter and whipped free.

"We're going in! Mayday mayday mayd—"

Street grabbed Alex Lupin and hurled him to the tarmac as a chunk of rotor blade snapped off and hit the wall next to where they were crouching. The helicopter made a whine like a struck cat, crashed against the side of the building just short of the helipad, then dropped like a stone.

Street and T.J. were the first to the edge of the roof, where they watched sickened and appalled as the chopper careened into the street, stopping in a gnarled heap in the middle of an intersection, twisting itself over twice before the fuel ignited. The spinning, along with the explosion, completely shredded and scattered the airframe. Rotor blades broke off and became high-profile shrapnel.

Free-flying rotor blades throttled the side of the building, then slashed into several police cars parked below. Another ripped through a kiosk in Pershing Square as the proprietor quite literally ran for his life.

Smoke, flame, and wreckage cluttered the street below. Street cranked backward so abruptly that he pulled a muscle in his back, and dragged Alex Lupin inside the building as Hondo and the others formed a protective ring around them.

Lupin, damn him, was smiling.

"Everyone okay?" Hondo asked.

Nobody answered, but a few miserable thumbs came up.

"This is Seventy-David," Hondo went on into the radio. "Open the door! We're coming back in!"

Inside the Parker Center, Captain Fuller approached once they were back in the Situation Room with a half dozen operations officers working telephones and keyboards. The L.A.P.D. brass around them looked downcast and beaten. And worried.

"What the hell happened?" Fuller demanded of Velasquez and Hondo and the team.

"Someone shot our bird down," Velasquez said.

"No shit! How?"

Hondo glanced at Street, because they both knew what he had to report. "Military high-explosive ammunition. Access to a .50-caliber weapon . . . that good a shot . . . we're dealing with someone elite. We're at a whole new level, Captain."

Not all cops had been soldiers. In fact, most, including Fuller, had never been in the service. They were perfectly fine police officers, though they might never have heard that weapon fired, or even seen one.

Fuller turned pink. "I want this Red Wolf asshole out of here now!"

Hondo calmly said, "Smart money says we keep him locked down here till we know who our threat is."

"I promised the chief I'd have this asshole outside city limits today! Is your team capable of executing that or not?"

Street hunkered down inside his collar, glad he wasn't the one who had to answer, because there was only one answer and he would feel silly giving it.

"Yes, sir," Hondo uttered by rote.

"Captain Fuller!" an officer called, and held out a phone receiver. "I've got the chief of police on the phone for you."

Fuller glared at him, then back at the team.

"Now we're talking about my ass! So draw up a plan, get him out of here, and do not screw it up!"

Brian Gamble casually retreated into his van in the parking garage and lowered the high-powered rifle from his shoulder. Beside him were wind charts of downtown, a barometer, and the enormous scope he'd just used.

"Nice shot," Travis told him from the driver's seat, still looking out at the column of smoke twisting upward from the downed helicopter.

Gamble wondered how many men he had just killed, then wondered at his own lack of care about them. He hadn't always been this way, but he sure was "this way" now. He didn't feel a ripple.

He shoved aside the foam baffles he had used to muffle the shot and crawled into the passenger seat beside Travis.

"Yeah," he said. "S.W.A.T. taught me how to do that."

14

A NEW BENTLEY PULLED UP TO THE RESTRICTED TARMAC where elite visitors boarded and debarked from private planes. A waiting Gulfstream private jet stood in elegant repose, gleaming as a handsome couple in their sixties emerged from the Bentley, assisted by their driver, who then hurried to get the luggage out of the luxury car's trunk. Elizabeth Segerstrom proudly accepted her husband's hand as she stepped onto the little stairway that would take them up to the new jet. The old one had lasted nearly twenty years, and this was finally the upgrade they had dreamed of.

The Segerstroms' lives had been one of dreams come true. They had started with almost nothing, better than forty years ago. They had been happy together, but unfulfilled. First one child fulfilled a dream, then four miscarriages before the next miracle occurred and they were jubilant. During the period of miscarriage after miscarriage, she and her husband had worked doggedly ten hours a day to build a business in the investment field. Now co-presidents of an international finance firm, they still occasionally thought of those four children they lost and how much happier they might have been spending money on those kids than just sinking it back into the business.

Then their son and daughter, the ones who had survived the whimsy of genetic doom, had thrown them a whopping anniversary party this year, and kindly included photographs of four babies—just any four babies—representing the sisters and brother who had not lived. Those babies were celebrated as tokens of the love between Beth and Richard Segerstrom, celebrated by their two children and nine grandchildren. Their son and daughter had gleefully declared in front of everyone present, at a party of over six hundred, that they had each decided early in life to have lots of kids as a way of giving their parents the love of many children who by rights should've been their own.

The Segerstroms had millions of dollars now, but would happily give them up to have raised those other four kids, yet all the millions were only cotton candy compared to the beautiful family with whom they were blessed to share this earth.

Basking in satisfaction and the bright pride on her husband's face, she stepped into the glossy airplane and discovered a small but tidy interior, lovely as the lobby of a fine hotel, done in the stone and sand colors of the desert, with microfiber suede curtains and plush carpet.

Today there was only one thing that could be construed as wrong or uneven . . . they both perfectly hated to fly. Since the terrorist attacks of 2001, they had harbored an uneasy twitch of nerves at the idea of getting in a plane. Oh, they both knew it was illogical, especially on a private aircraft. In fact, they were in more danger driving to the airport.

But they were wealthy and they were busy. The two factors simply did not add up to a car trip.

Mrs. Segerstrom looked around in approval as her husband answered a cell phone call, and a moment later was greeted by a young lady pilot, or co-pilot.

"Good afternoon, Mrs. Segerstrom," the new girl said.

"Talk to them," Richard Segerstrom barked from the top of the air stairs. "Try to make it work. I really don't need another problem today."

Beth sighed to relax herself as her husband clicked his phone off, peeked into the cockpit, and looked at the two replacement pilots.

"Where's Mike?" he asked.

"Family emergency," the male pilot said from inside the cockpit. "Let me know if there's anything you need."

Mrs. Segerstrom handed her tote bag to the female, the co-pilot. "Just get us there alive, for starters."

Everyone accommodated her with a laugh. They all liked her right away. She was that kind of person.

Now for some clear sailing.

PARKER CENTER GARAGE

Twenty S.W.A.T. officers prepared their gear and weapons for the alternative transport method. Ass and elbows, mostly. Vehicles—police Suburbans and black-and-whites—were being readied all around them, preparing to caravan out of Los Angeles. The cruisers were packed with officers.

Hondo gave his own squad a once-over. He was nervous. They could all tell, and they were nervous too. Somebody had clearly set them up to have to transport by ground. The chances that this would be an incident-free transfer was very small now.

"A hundred million buys a lot of trouble," Hondo was saying, more or less the end of a long solid grumble since the helicopter went down. "Everyone knows what they have to do?" When they each nodded, he bleated, "Where the hell's T.J.?"

T.J. came running up then and heard the question. "Bad Thai food. Had to make a head call."

"You good to go?"

"I'm fine."

"All right," Hondo said. "Let's make the captain look like a hero."

*   *   *

Alex, alone in his cell, looked up from where he sat. Boxer and Sanchez approached, their expressions unreadable. "Time to go," Boxer said to him.

"Mount up!" Sergeant Howard called out. "Move it! We're rolling!"

Heavy doors thudded closed, creating a drumming echo in the garage. Vehicles began to pull out, in a prescribed order.

Outside, riot cops stalked the perimeter. Barricades were rolled back to let the cavalcade process. You'd think the Pope was being moved from here to there.

Or Al Capone, maybe. Much closer.

Vehicle after vehicle pulled out of the garage with the black Suburban in the center. Police motorcycles leapfrogged ahead to clock intersections. Citizens had crowded the sidewalks, including some women with MARRY ME, ALEX signs. Wonder who was making money selling those signs? Some entrepreneurs sure were quick thinkers. Anybody who filled a need that fast deserved every dollar. One of the women pulled up her skirt as the Suburban passed by, and gave the attendees a good flash.

Such class.

The convoy made good, steady progress, moving along at a decent but safe and planned clip, pushing the speed limit in every area, though not going so much over it that there might be a chance of losing control or being surprised by vehicles in intersections. The motorcycle cops continued anticipating traffic and heading it off, though driveways and garages were hard to predict.

They moved east, through downtown into an industrial area with truck and rail facilities.

This area was less nerve–wracking than the closed-in urban and suburban areas they'd passed through. There was more opportunity here for a long-range sniper, but the vehicles were armored and the windows were tinted. Even the sharpest shooter would have trouble getting a bead on a particular person, and how would that help anyway? Nobody wanted to kill Lupin, especially not anyone who wanted his money.

Killing the cops wouldn't do anything in a convoy this big. Other cops would just swarm in to take their places.

No, a rifle wouldn't be the way anymore.

Everything had been preplanned. There was already a plan in place for this kind of transport. Each vehicle knew the order it was supposed to be in, and its particular job in the procession. The method had been developed long ago for the purposes of transporting VIPs, escorting government vehicles with high-exposure personnel in them—presidents, princes, sheiks, Princess Diana, movie stars, Elvis . . . L.A.P.D had seen them all.

And, yes, even transporting high-profile prisoners now and then, fancy that. Yes, once in a while the cops even did something that involved crime. The Al Capones and John Gottis of the world once in a while had to be moved around, and the system had to be in place and screwed down to do it right.

So nobody was particularly worried. They had all the upper hands, and they were all edgy and ticked because of the deaths of the helicopter personnel and the prison bus guards. Angry and insulted policemen were nothing to be tampered with.

The unspoken agreement was that if anyone was going to kill Alex Lupin, it would be one of the police officers. No one had come out with an order, exactly, or even a hazy plan, but it was the nature of all these uniformed and plainclothes officers that they knew the dangers of letting Alex Lupin escape. Better one of them take him out than allow a crime boss of such power and notoriety to be once again free, to let someone out there in a smelling devious world profit from so diabolical an action as freeing Lupin. If a hundred million dollars changed hands in an international criminal community, the balance of power would change too. Suddenly there would be new bosses and new problems.

Not to mention . . . there would also be the terrible precedent of Lupin's offer. If it succeeded, such offers would be unstoppable and common. Law enforcement all over the world would suddenly be dealing with thousands of daring highest bidders.

The whole prospect was too ugly.

All at once, three cars in front of the Suburban, an eighteen-wheeled semitrailer pulled down a side street. It gained speed, accelerating steadily, with such a roar that its engine could be heard inside every car of the convoy—and that was a lot of loud.

The officers in the Suburban saw the square nose of the tractor-trailer just as it smashed through a chain-link fence—the only barrier between it and the convoy.

The motorcycle cops had ignored the truck because of the chain-link fence!

Before anyone could digest more than that, the truck howled across the road lanes and nailed a squad car two ahead of the Suburban, bulldozing the car across the lanes and right into the concrete meridian. Now the tractor-trailer blocked off the entire street, cutting the head of the convoy off from the rest.

Brakes screeched hideously. Tire smoke wafted as four lanes of traffic scratched to a halt in chaotic order. The convoy turned into a giant accordion.

The Suburban tried to shift into reverse and gun out of the way, but it was caught between the big rig and the vehicles of the rearguard.

Good—the rearguard was already reacting, already backing up, trying to clear the way. The Suburban would have room to turn around in just a few seconds.

Being ready for something, expecting something, didn't necessarily mean all would go the right way. The cops couldn't have known what the "something" would be, so no one expected a second tractor-trailer to come bombing out of the same side street. This one veered so abruptly that for a second it seemed the truck might turn itself over, but it didn't. It held a course in a prescribed choreography, slamming a patrol car two vehicles behind the Suburban.

The trap was sprung. The Suburban and one other patrol car were now caught, alone, cut off from the vanguard and the rearguard of the motorcade. They were only just now getting the idea of how much a hundred million dollars really was.

They got a little better idea when the second tractor-trailer opened up its giant side door and a full dozen assault troops poured out, wearing gas masks.

Why did they need—

The question answered itself, sharply, shockingly, when gas grenades rained from the building on the west side of the street, high up on one of the balconies. Nobody saw which balcony, and by the time they thought to look, the street was enshrouded in a thick fog. The bad guys had given themselves all the advantages.

The maneuver was as flawless and timed as any S.W.A.T. maneuver. Obviously there were military minds at work, but not military hearts. No American soldier with any pride left would abuse his talents and the training freely given to him by the American taxpayers to compromise the system that had given him everything.

Clearly, though, there were enough corrupted souls out there to distort that happy assumption.

The assault team carried the terrorist's weapon of

choice—AK-47s—and they weren't shy about using them.

But the three cops in the patrol car didn't wait. They opened fire with M-16s, and the battle was on. One assaulter was hit right off, dead before he could collect a dime. Wonder what he had been promised?

Rather than take their comrade's cue and bug out, realizing they were the stooges in a much bigger game, the tunnel-visioned bad guys also opened fire, making the bet that they would be the ones to survive. The patrol car became the preferred target, and took multiple hits.

One bold gangster jumped up on the hood of the Suburban, aimed his AK down at the windshield, and jackhammered the armored glass. AK slugs tore deep into the shielded material.

"Open this shit right now!" the gas-masked perp shouted.

Trapped, with the windshield a field of crackled divots, the cop inside simply pushed the Unlock button and let the bad guys in.

He could do that, because he was fully body-armored, and the Suburban was otherwise completely empty.

The gangster jumped off the hood, looking inside, and cursed a purple streak.

He backed away from the false target, only to find himself and his fellow assault team slammed to the ground by L.A.P.D. and S.W.A.T. officers who seemed to come out of nowhere in swarms.

Whatever these animals had been promised, they'd have a hard time spending it.

While the convoy was being assaulted and had done its job of distracting attention, Hondo, Street, and the new team were dragging Alex Lupin through an underground tunnel. It was a secret way out of the Parker Center. Lupin was shackled and wearing Kevlar over his county jail jumpsuit. They were at the stairs that led outside.

Out there, two low-profile cars awaited the team. Hondo, Deke, and Sanchez climbed into the first car. T.J. drove the second, with Street, Boxer, and Lupin riding. Off they went, into the descending night.

Street rode in the passenger seat, ironically "shotgun," since he was holding his rifle right on his lap.

"My sister's been dating some new guy," Boxer said from the backseat.

For a moment Street didn't say anything, but then decided to go with it.

"Yeah?"

"Met him for the first time the other night."

Generously Street said, "Well, good for her."

"Nah . . . he's an asshole." Boxer paused for a moment. "Maybe you should give her a call. Y'know . . . if you want."

Street hid a smile. Boxer was all the way into I'm-sorry mode now. It was nice to hear.

"Okay," Street obliged. "Yeah, maybe I will."

They went silent as the radio buzzed and there was a message from Hondo, talking from the first car.

"Seventy-David to Ten-David."

"Seventy-David, I just got word that the convoy was hit."

"Jesus Christ, what was the damage?"

"Jerry Fargas is dead and two patrolmen are on the operating table at Drew King."

Street exchanged a glance with T.J. as they tensed and listened.

"Is there an ID on the suspects?"

"Roger, three rival gangs came together. Money over colors, I guess."

"What's your twenty, Ten-David?"

"Right on top of you."

"That's good to know. T.J., pay attention back there. They're coming out of the woodwork."

T.J. didn't answer.

Probably choked up, mad. Street was mad too, and turned to sear a look into Alex Lupin.

The racketeer was unflinching. "American greed," he commented. "So predictable."

"Shut up, asshole," Street said. "An officer's dead because you shot your mouth off."

"That's how I like cops. Dead."

"Want to join him?"

"He knew the dangers," Lupin casually dictated. "That's probably why he signed up to be a police officer. To carry a gun in the Wild West."

A few seconds passed in silence. No one wanted to engage this man in conversation. There was a certain prudence. It was unwise to let a master criminal get a good look, weld their voices into his mind, be able to identify them after the edge had come off the memory of this day. They wanted to be just pawns of the system to him, not individuals who deserved his revenge. Those things could happen.

So they kept quiet.

Lupin didn't.

"Would you be sitting here if this job wasn't dangerous?" he prodded. "Or isn't it really what you live for? Killing that cop probably got you twenty new recruits. You should thank me."

"You're right" popped out of Street. "Boxer, thank him for me."

Boxer offered Alex Lupin a gesture of kindness right in the ribs. He doubled and came up coughing. While he fought to shake off the assault, Street winked at Boxer.

"Checkpoint One is on the left," Hondo's voice informed them.

T.J. spoke to the voice-activated mike. "Roger, Hondo, I see it."

They had the radios open, so they could hear one another talking.

"Sanchez," they heard Deke say, "you are hardcore. You been watching every person we pass like a hawk on the hunt."

"Hands," Sanchez's voice was faint. "I'm watching everyone's hands. Empty hand, no weapon. I'm going home to my girl, Deke."

"And I'm going home to my brats too."

Then they heard Hondo comment, "I got a deer to feed. Stand by for Checkpoint Two."

In the second car T.J. was tense as he turned at the second checkpoint.

Boxer must've seen something, because he said, "Relax, T.J. Hondo transported the President like this in 'ninety-six. Nobody had a clue."

"That was Clinton," Street pointed out. "Nobody cared."

"I can double my offer," Lupin said then. Maybe he sensed hope slipping away and wanted to catch it. "Sixty-six million for each of you. All you have to do is let me go right here. I'll find my own way home."

"Okay, sure," Street said. "You got the cash on you? 'Cuz we don't take a check."

"Be smart about this," Lupin suggested. "What do you make? Sixty-six thousand a year?"

"Not even with overtime."

"Checkpoint Three. Making our turn."

Ahead of them the first car made what appeared to be a fairly leisurely turn to the right and went briefly out of sight behind the corner building.

T.J. should've begun his turn. Street watched as the intersection approached. Only when T.J. made no effort to aim toward the new angle did Street look at him.

At the look, T.J. slammed on the brakes. Street was thrown forward against the dash. When he recovered, his shoulder screaming, T.J. had a gun to his face.

"You move," T.J. whispered with a hiss, "you die."

15

WHILE HIS ASTONISHED TEAMMATES LOOKED ON, T.J. McCabe clicked off the voice-activation and used the mike.

"Pedestrian in the crosswalk, Hondo. I'll be on your tail in ten seconds."

"Ten-four."

From the backseat Alex Lupin was the only one in the car who was calm. "Looks like my ride is here."

"T.J.," Street began, his heart in a knot, "what are you doing?"

"Making history," T.J. said. "And a little coin."

Street had managed to turn slightly sideways in the seat, enough to get Boxer in his periphery and keep an eye on Lupin. Before he could think of anything to do, how to handle this, some way to move that T.J. wouldn't already have thought of, Boxer's hand made a surreptitious movement toward his own gun.

The car exploded. Or it seemed to—the rear window was blown out by a shotgun blast that took Boxer out in a shower of blood.

Feeling Boxer slump against the back of his seat, Jim Street sucked a ragged breath and held his hands up.

"Damn it!" T.J. blurted. "Why'd you shoot him!"

A face appeared in the passenger-side window as T.J. lowered the glass panel.

Jim Street didn't want to accept what he saw behind the shadow of stubble at his side. He knew resentment could burrow deep, but this was all the way to hell.

Brian Gamble leaned down to look inside the car through the window at Street's side. "He was going for his piece. How 'bout you, Jim? Want to be a cowboy?"

Street just glared. What was there to say? Were there more questions to ask? How bad can a cop go when he goes bad? Things like that?

He wanted desperately to help Boxer. Men had survived bad wounds before, hadn't they? Knives in the chest, bullets in the head, the heart . . .

But Boxer's telltale gurgle had gone away. Possibly Street had just imagined that it had been there at all. He thought about Boxer's wife, his hopes and future. They'd been bright until this past thirty seconds, until they were disintegrated by a former police officer who had once taken an oath to be a bulwark against crime and this kind of horror.

Now Brian Gamble was the very face of that horror. Embittered and self-serving, there was nothing left of the honorable cause or the oath sworn.

"T.J.? Street? Car Two, acknowledge."

T.J. raised the mike again, but this time his voice was rough and unpleasant. "Catching up to you, Sarge. We'll be there in—"

"Hondo, Code Four!" Street shouted.

A hard force slammed him in the chin. The butt of Gamble's shotgun.

Too late. Hondo had heard, Street was sure of it as he came up, bleeding from the mouth.

"Flip a bitch!"

"Flipping."

They were coming. They'd gotten the call. Street could almost hear the screech of Hondo, Deke, and Sanchez's car tires, though his mind rang and his jaw throbbed. The siren would be going on too, and the emergency light would be slapped on top of the otherwise plainclothes car.

Sanchez might say a prayer, the way her mother did when they got their first call.

"Affirmative. Car Two has stopped on top of Bunker Hill."

That was the voice of Lieutenant Velasquez, high up in the helicopter they'd arranged for as secondary surveillance. Street got a rush of satisfaction that they had been spotted from the air, and now there was no way to lose a chopper that had them in its sights.

But it was night . . . wasn't it? Street tried to remember. His brain was washing back and forth inside his head. He'd been hit pretty hard.

He heard a click behind him and registered slowly that Gamble must be unlocking Lupin's shackles. A siren . . . was that in his throbbing head?

whopwhopwhopwhopwhopwhop

Sounded like a retread flopping on pavement.

No . . . helicopter blades. Good. Wasn't it good? Yeah, it was good. . . .

His eyes cleared a little, and he realized he hadn't been able to see anything for a few . . . seconds or minutes? Dark tunnel vision widened. The steering wheel. His hand . . . he was cuffed to the wheel.

"Do me a favor, Jimmy."

Hmm? Gamble's voice.

"Tell Fuller it was me who pulled this off."

Street shook away the grogginess with sheer will. "I ain't letting you pull it off."

"You don't got a say in the matter."

Street twisted enough to find Gamble's eyes and fix on them. "You start running," he warned, "you better not stop."

Gamble's eyes turned mellow for an instant. Then the hardness returned.

"Ten-four, partner," he said. "T.J., let's move."

T.J. pulled Alex Lupin from the car, and the three of them struck off running.

Street's full strength flowed back as he fought the cuffs that trapped him to the wheel like a cat tied to a post. It was futile.

"Boxer!" he shouted. "Come on, Boxer! Wake up!"

He heard gunshots and only then realized that his M-4 was missing. He fished around on the floor with one foot. Nothing.

Then the sound he'd just heard clicked in his head and he remembered. Street knew that sound and it wasn't a shotgun. Gamble must've taken his M-4!

The sound of the helicopter in the air made a sharp surge and roared in a whole other way than the noise it had been making before. So they were shooting at the chopper. With his gun!

"Ten-David to 114! Two assailants have commandeered our prisoner at Hill and Sixth! All suspects are wearing S.W.A.T. clothing and have automatic weapons."

Street tried to twist again. His wrist was starting to bleed from rubbing against the handcuffs. He saw a face out the window and realized a motorist in a blue car had pulled up and was staring at them.

"Call 911!" he shrieked. "Call 911!"

But the guy got a funny look on his face and sped off into the night.

"Shit. Boxer! Wake up!"

To his shock, he was rewarded with a little gurgle. And Boxer was moving! Now there was a moan—a sign of life!

"Boxer, stay with me. It's not over, I swear to God!" He yanked the cuffs again, punishing himself.

231

Just then Deke came careening through oncoming traffic, light flashing, siren howling, and three angry persons inside. Their brakes locked up as they fishtailed to a stop. The doors popped open and all three S.W.A.T. members piled out to converge on Car Number 2 and Jim Street, who was never so glad to see anybody in his life. Over the car's radio came Velasquez's muffled voice: "All suspects are wearing body armor and have automatic weapons—"

"It was T.J. and Gamble!" Street gasped. "They're going down to the subway."

The astonished three looked at Boxer in the backseat, slumped and bleeding, then Hondo recovered and uncuffed Street.

"Come on," Hondo said. "You two take care of Boxer."

He bolted off running, with Street right beside him.

"Get the kit!" they heard Sanchez tell Deke. The first-aid kit in the other car. Over Hondo's personal radio unit they heard the rest. "Seventy-David. I need an RA unit at Hope and Fourth Street for an officer with a gunshot wound! Deke, put pressure on the wound!"

Boxer was getting help.

Let it not be too late. . . .

Overhead, the whine of the chopper changed again. A new direction. "Seventy-David. Suspects have entered the Pershing Square MTA station!"

"Roger, Ten-David," Hondo panted back as he

and Street changed direction toward the subway station.

The subway—the chopper couldn't keep an eye on them down there, damn it.

And there were dozens if not hundreds of innocent pedestrians down there. Or had Gamble arranged to take over the subway car?

Street thought Gamble might do something like that, just to increase his edge. That meant there were other people involved than just Gamble and T.J. He scoured his mind and came up with the guy in the pool hall. Gamble had called him by name . . .

"Leave it alone . . . Travis."

That was it. Travis.

Street made an inward bet that this guy was involved some way. He had been playing pool with Gamble, and Brian Gamble had never made friends easily. His list of cohorts would be short.

He and Hondo flew down the stairwell into the subway station in time to see the train open its throttle, scratch against the rails, and hum toward the tunnel.

T.J. gone bad . . . had he always been bad?

No, Alex Lupin had just dangled the carrot yesterday.

His stomach soured, Street ran like lightning alongside the subway car where he could see Lupin, T.J., and Gamble inside. They saw him too, and Hondo not far behind.

Gamble waved a casual bye-bye. Smug son of a bitch!

Always one step behind me, Gamble would be thinking.

Goddamn, I can still read his mind.

"Suspects are heading northbound on Train 1432 to Metro Center and Seventh and Figueroa!" Hondo shouted into his radio.

"Roger, Seventy-David."

"Dispatch, have Metro stop that train at the next station!"

Street's mind went in two directions. Did the paramedics have their hands on Boxer yet? Would Deke and Sanchez be able to join the chase? Maybe head off the train?

He slid down onto the track, with Hondo right behind, and started running through the tunnel as the train took on a muffled murmur deep underground and pulled away from them.

"You can't take that train to Mexico!" he shouted, and ran even faster.

Black-and-white squad cars converged on the next subway station. Police officers rushed down the stairs, pistols drawn, as Deke and Sanchez pulled up in their car and rushed down there too. The other cops deferred to them because of their S.W.A.T. uniforms, and Deke felt special.

Sanchez had done a good job with Boxer. She had done the best job of first-aid Deke had seen in a long time. Yeah, they were all trained in first-aid and CPR, but it was a whole other thing to use it on your own partner. She had kept her cool and done the job.

Now he was in the hands of the trauma teams. Would he make it? Survive an assault by another trained S.W.A.T. officer who had turned evil?

Funny . . . "evil" was supposed to be something in fairy tales, in kids' movies, in fantasy.

It existed, though. It did.

"Where the hell's this train!" Deke shouted.

A uniformed officer beside him said, "Should've been here by now."

They paused, listened.

Sanchez shot him a glance, then spoke into her radio. "Hondo, the train never made it to Figueroa!"

Deke spun to the uniformed officers around them. "Secure this station!"

Then he jumped down onto the tracks, with Sanchez on his heels. Together they tore into the dark black tunnel.

16

Street picked up his pace. He felt Hondo do the same close behind and marveled that he, a trained and disciplined runner, could be matched by sheer adrenaline and bottom rage. He felt Hondo's anger and insult at what had happened. It matched his own, especially about Boxer. That shot was unnecessary.

Gamble had completely flipped, but in a dangerously sane way. All his humanity was gone. All that was left, it seemed, must be the hardened trainee who knew all the cops' tricks and all the tricks of soldiering. If those were not tempered with honor and conscience, the leached-out remains could be the most ferocious weapon in the world. That's what had created history's greatest evils—Stalin, Hitler, Caesar, Saddam. They had power, and they just didn't care.

Now there was Brian Gamble. All right, he didn't command armies or nations or the hearts of misguided millions. Or would he, by the end of the month?

What could a hundred million dollars really do in

the wrong hands? The proposition was scary, and huge, he told himself. Saddam and Stalin had started with less. Twisted minds could twist pretty far.

Brian had been distilled down to the chaff. There was nothing left of the officer and gentleman Jim Street admired and trusted. Seemed impossible to go so very bad from so very good. Street couldn't get his mind around it.

He was a police officer, though, and evidence spoke for itself. If there had been anything worth saving in Brian Gamble an hour ago, that chance for soul rescue had been shot away with the assault on Boxer.

They were still sprinting at full throttle, barely breathing heavily, when they spotted the MTA subway car stopped on the tracks in front of them. They slowed to come around the bend, weapons at the ready, and came to a cautious prowl.

A foot scraped somewhere in the tunnel. Street tensed even more.

"Police! Freeze! Put your hands behind your head!"

It was an MTA engineer. The man came out of a shadow, scared stiff and not sure just whom he was facing this time.

"Where are they?" Street demanded.

Terrified, the engineer simply pointed to a sewer drain.

Then more pounding of feet—Street shifted his aim, but it was only Sanchez and Deke arriving from the other station.

"Where are they?" Sanchez asked.

"Seventy-David to Ten-David," Hondo said into his radio, "suspects have entered an air vent approximately a quarter mile north of Metro Center. Accessing that vent now."

"Roger, Seventy-David. We'll deploy above the ground accordingly."

It was Lieutenant Velasquez, sounding tight and mean.

Street felt clammy and hot as he stepped into the drain . . . vent . . . hole in the earth . . . hind butt-hole of California . . . window to the future . . . shaft to hell . . .

PARKER CENTER SITUATION ROOM

Captain Fuller watched a couple of city engineers measure and study blueprints of the vast underground infrastructure beneath Los Angeles. Might as well be the catacombs of Rome.

"Somebody tell me something!" he bellowed. "Where are they going?"

"Pretty much anywhere they want," the nearest engineer said, a little embarrassed as well as frustrated. "This shaft intersects with the storm drain system. They can pop up out of any manhole in a five-mile radius."

"How many manholes are we talking about?"

The engineer glanced at another guy, then admitted, "Six thousand."

Fuller clenched his fists till they hurt. "I can't cover six thousand manhole covers."

The engineers shifted around, peering again at the blueprints as if some magic red line might appear to indicate the path of the escapees. A minor traffic offense had blown up into an international incident, and now it had metamorphosed into something even more complex—the awful unpredictable. No one could predict what wounds would fester into virulent infections of crime because of this influx of new money, not to mention the abrupt freedom of Alexander Lupin.

Lupin's whole way of doing business would change now that he had been so thoroughly exposed. All the law-enforcement and Interpol activity focusing on Lupin and his crime network would be useless. He would change all his tactics, his locations, his contacts, he entire business. Undercover officers who were well entrenched might actually be killed as part of a culling process. In fact, it was chillingly probable.

"R-Commander," Fuller spoke into the desk mike, "get out of that airship, set up a command post at Sixth and Olive, and give me a land-line, Code Two."

"Roger that, Captain," Velasquez responded from somewhere. "We've got confirmation on our suspects."

"Who are they?" Fuller's question came through a tight set of gritted teeth.

"Former Officer Gamble working with Officer T. J. McCabe."

Fuller's stomach fell. "You gotta be shittin' me. . . . Gamble, as in Street's ex-partner?"

Bile rose in his throat at the idea. He had never liked those guys, but—what they hell difference did that make? Had he hated them right into this?

No! Interdepartmental friction was no excuse!

"Affirmative."

Velasquez's answer had taken a few seconds longer than necessary.

"We got two trained S.W.A.T. guys leading this attack?" Captain Fuller had to hear the words out loud as the concept solidified in his head. "How do we know the rest of the team isn't in on it with them?"

"Because I can vouch for Hondo."

Fuller grimaced. "Would you bet a hundred million on it?" he challenged.

Velasquez didn't answer.

Fuller turned to the desk sergeant. "Have we reestablished radio contact with Hondo's team?"

The sergeant shook his head. No, they hadn't. It wasn't what Fuller needed to hear.

No sounds from Hondo. Could the ugly truth be even uglier than he now suspected? Uglier than Velasquez's faith in Dan "Hondo" Harrelson?

He knew what he had to do, and though he had resisted reinstating Street, exonerating Gamble, bringing Hondo back, the whole package, a sickening sensation came into his entire body as he gave the command he knew he had to give.

"Put Central Bureau on tactical alert," he ordered.

*　　*　　*

Street maneuvered down the drippy, dark tunnel with Hondo and the others backing him up. They shifted now and then to be sure they were covering one another completely. They knew their enemy, and their enemy was themselves—S.W.A.T. echoes, with S.W.A.T. training and S.W.A.T. reflexes. They couldn't assume a damned thing. Their enemy also knew them.

"Seventy-David to Ten-David," Hondo attempted again.

There hadn't been a radio response in almost five minutes. No signal down here in hell.

"Seventy-David to Ten-David, you copy?"

The sensation of aloneness doubled on itself. They felt as if they were exploring an alien planet.

"Greg?" Hondo called. "You there? R-Commander? Seventy-David, radio check."

Nothing. A second or two later Hondo hurried to catch up with Street.

Street felt his sergeant's tension as if lines of electricity were connecting the two of them.

"No reception down here," Hondo said.

Street paused, keeping his eyes forward, and whispered the tactical scheme. "Gamble wants us on an island."

Hondo digested that concept. So they were being steered, led, maneuvered into seclusion. A trap.

"All right," Hondo accepted. "Heads up, people. Expect anything."

"He's got some kind of plan," Street murmured. "He's probably marked off his path with duct tape or something that peels up so he won't leave the same trail for us. He knows exactly where he's going, and he's leaving us down here in the maze, out of touch." He paused, trying to sort out everything that had happened so far and force it all into order. "Hondo, they must know it was Gamble by now."

"Yeah, they do. So what?"

Street looked at him, or what there was of him shaded in the darkness. "And T.J."

"Yeah. What's your point?"

"We can't contact anybody. Gamble probably knew there's no signal down here. He would've checked it out. Our silence isn't gonna sound very good to Fuller."

"You mean they might think . . ."

"Wouldn't you?"

"Hell, no!" Hondo paused. A moment later he grumbled, "Hell, yes . . . shit, shit, shit."

Suddenly they didn't know who would be shooting at them, or from what direction. And they didn't dare return fire on uniformed officers, because T.J., Gamble, and even Alex Lupin were wearing S.W.A.T. gear now, just to throw them off.

Street moved back to the point position. Sanchez and Deke brought up the rear. Their nerves were now tipped with explosives. They could feel one another's presence like electrical charges crackling between their bodies.

Another fork in the tunnel . . . which way?

He looked down, trying to see maybe a dry spot

or some leftover tape, or a string that comes on the edge of duct tape when you rip it just wrong.

Nothing.

He kept moving, with nothing but instinct to follow.

Another fork. Brian Gamble ripped his duct-taped arrow off the wall as Lupin, Travis, and T.J. kept moving forward down the correct tunnel. He had impressed Lupin with his thoroughness. Somehow that wasn't much of a compliment, though.

He didn't care, really, what Lupin thought as long as the bastard was good for the money. There had been some satisfaction in the shock he saw in Jim Street's face, but his hand still itched at the prospect of having shot the other officer. He didn't feel bad, exactly. Every police officer signed up to maybe get shot. It was part of the job. Still, something in him twitched a little. Just habit, probably.

"Hold up," he said when he got to the right spot. "Stay right on me. No one touch anything."

He led the group to the right, searching the tunnel ahead. There were discarded loading pallets and some trash blocking the way. He stopped, surveyed it, then motioned the others on past the heaped mess.

"Walk there," he said, pointing the way through. "Watch your step. Keep moving. I'll catch up."

He moved the pallets and uncovered a couple of

small military mines. He set the explosives and made sure the detonators were just right, then popped a smoke grenade and ran to join the others up ahead.

"They'll be dead before they even know they're in trouble," he told them.

Travis shook his head. "You're a sick puppy, man."

T.J. was hot and bitter. "This was supposed to be a snatch-and-extract operation! You didn't say anything about shooting cops! Boxer was my friend!"

Alex Lupin came to Gamble's rescue with his own cold version of reality.

"You can buy new friends," he said.

T.J. blew his top, shoving Lupin up against a wall with his M-4 to the racketeer's head.

"You don't want to mess with me!" he ground out. "I just crossed a line. I don't mind crossing another one."

Lupin smiled. How many times in his life had he had a gun to his head?

"What are you going to do?" he challenged. "Shoot me?"

T.J. said nothing, did nothing.

So Lupin laughed and looked at Gamble. "He's slowing us down. Give me your gun. I'll take care of him."

Gamble frowned with complete distaste. There were lines to cross, that was for sure, but who in hell needed to cross every single one of them?

"Shut up and keep moving," he said. "Or I'll shoot both of you."

Lupin didn't move. "If I die, you get nothing."

Gamble ignored him. "Let's go, T.J."

Nothing changed. T.J. didn't move. So Lupin, cocky bastard that he was, put his mouth on T.J.'s gun muzzle and grinned around the metal like a jackass clown.

T.J. seethed visibly, ready to pull the trigger.

Gamble didn't move. "T.J. . . . please take the gun out of his mouth."

A few weird seconds passed, until T.J. finally pulled the gun back. What else could he do at this point?

"Thank you," Gamble said. "Let's keep moving."

Every few dozen feet, he stopped to listen back into the tunnel. No boom yet.

"You hear something?" Alex Lupin asked on the third pause.

"Nope. That's the problem. Come on. We gotta go."

He suddenly felt urgent and pushed Lupin ahead to a grate marked with a duct-taped *X*. He ripped off the tape, then banged on the cover with the butt of his gun.

"Nick! You there, man?"

"Who's Nick?" Lupin asked casually, as if they were discussing a baseball game.

"Former Delta Force. Don't tick him off."

"Oh, sure." Lupin was perfectly smug. He was making fun of them and not hiding his self-satisfaction at all.

The grate scraped off with a heavy metallic sound. A rough-hewn face peered down at them.

"You smell like shit," the man said.

"Yeah, it's a sewer," Gamble plainly told him. "Where's our air?"

"On track. On schedule."

Nick reached down to help them all out of the tunnel, into a whole new life, then handed Gamble a radio.

"Air Unit One," Gamble called, "what's your status?"

"We're approximately forty-five miles due east of Point Bravo. We've begun our descent. Six-minute ETA."

"Roger that."

Travis and Nick closed the grate, then secured it with a heavy industrial lock, while T.J. escorted Alex Lupin to the back of a hauntingly familiar black Suburban.

"Van One, Van Two," Gamble addressed into the radio, "you guys got five minutes. Copy that?"

"Roger. Five minutes."

"Van Two. We copy that."

He hopped into the driver's seat, reveling in the sounds of his new network of operatives. A hundred million bucks could sure buy a lot of loyalty, he thought.

Five minutes to freedom, wealth, power, and glory. Not bad for a day's work.

"All units in the vicinity of the Hawthorne Airport, residents report beacon lights turned on after closing hours."

"Dispatch, R-Commander. Deploy all available units to the Hawthorne Airport." Fuller looked then as the desk sergeant and added, "Call the FAA for details."

"Ten-four, Commander."

He looked up as Agent Hauser from the FBI crossed to him with a cup of coffee. What in hell kind of moron wanted coffee at a time like this? Typical Feds—too much of an eye on the big picture and never bothering to watch the pieces.

"They're going to fly him out of the country, goddamn it," Hauser said.

Fuller ignored him. "R-Commander, Ten-David. Get you and your people out there!"

"Roger, sir," Velasquez responded from the helicopter, now probably making a U-turn back toward Hawthorne. "Perimeter established around airport. Additional S.W.A.T. units are en route."

"Copy that, Ten-David. Any word from Hondo's team?"

"No, advised Seventy-David is still out of radio contact."

That was Velasquez's way of sticking up for his new team, his old friend, and people they had both counted on. That was a way of giving them the benefit of the doubt. "Out of contact." Like they were maybe stuck in a lead vault.

No word. Not a whimper. Dead silence didn't make a good sound in this situation.

Fuller smelled betrayal.

He leaned on the desk and muttered, "Hondo, you son of a bitch . . ."

Jim Street followed every instinct he could dredge up, every old hint, every scabbed-over sensation or guess he knew about Brian Gamble's way of planning and thinking, and he led his team with a thin flashlight beam.

He'd given up on the floor. Too moist. There was no dependable way to leave a trail. Within a few dozen feet he found what he was feeling along for—a place on the wall where the grime had been scraped or peeled off. He raised his flashlight, moved it slowly along the wall, and discovered the faint outline of a crude arrow shape.

"This way," he said with a touch of victory.

"Stay close," Hondo warned, keeping everyone toward the wall Street was searching.

"What's that?" Hondo asked, pointing ahead.

"Smoke," Street said. "Perfect."

Grim gray smoke obscured their way, but it also told him they were on the right track. Gamble had let off a smoke bomb or something to confuse them, without realizing that the smoke was a perfect telltale road sign.

"Looks like we're gonna have to do this by Braille," Hondo commented, but he sounded hopeful.

Street didn't comment. He was moving ahead largely by feel now, and a few other inner signals. His hands and also his feet shimmied along, and he was aware of even the slightest—

Deke was beside him, pressing on the other wall. Street suddenly lunged for him, tackling him in a body-long attack and driving him backward. They hit the nasty ground side by side.

"Jesus Christ, Jimbo—" Deke gulped.

"Trip wire!" Street pointed out a thin line leading to a—"Live mine."

The mine was arranged under part of an old rotted pallet. It and the surrounding mess of trash would've turned into shrapnel and cut them all to pieces if that thing had gone off.

Hondo peered at it.

"Claymore," he decided. "Nasty shit."

Street pulled Deke to his feet.

"Old Indian saying," Hondo continued. "Where there's one white man, there's more white men."

"Splashes on the wall," Street pointed out. "They walked this way. Stay behind me."

Then he got behind Hondo, as kind of a nod to who was really in command.

Hondo led them around the mine. They carefully put their feet in the same spots where his had been, until they were all past the point of danger.

At least, this point of danger. Certainly there would be more coming up.

And they found it. The only grate leading out of this tunnel where Deke almost tripped the mine. Locked, with a mother of a lock.

"Well, ain't this a bitch," Hondo commented.

"A cold hard one," Street agreed, peering upward. "You got any ideas?"

"Sure."

"Want to share one or two?"

"I'm a very sharing guy, Sarge."

Luckily, Gamble had provided a solution—an undetonated Claymore.

"Careful," Street suggested as he and Deke gingerly transported the unexploded supernova to a place where it would do them some good.

"No shit," Deke agreed.

Within three minutes Street was jury-rigging the mine to the manhole as the team lurked around, watching him work. He had asked them all to step back, out of the blast funnel, but they refused to leave him. Didn't make any sense, but it was decent and certainly heartwarming.

Could've been just the light of betrayal shining on some real integrity, but their steadfastness as he took his big risk made Street feel better.

"You know what you're doing?" Hondo asked him.

"Remember when you asked me what I did in the Seals?"

"Yeah . . ."

Street shrugged his shoulders by way of an answer and dropped back down to the floor. "Cover," he suggested.

They ran like hell down the tunnel to what they hoped was a safe distance. Safe from the actual explosion, maybe. Was it safe from the concussion and shock wave?

He hoped so. A tunnel was a bad place to light off a bomb, like being caught in the barrel of a gun when the hammer falls. They couldn't afford to be stunned, even for a few minutes. Not even for a few seconds.

"Plug your ears," he said, and aimed his gun at the mine.

BAAAFOOOOOOOM

They were free. Okay, deaf, but free.

They ran through the clog of new smoke to the grate and found it completely missing. They climbed out just in time to see the grate return to earth from fifty feet in the air. The metallic bang chimed down the street.

Hondo clapped Street on the back, and they were running. Weapons engaged, they scanned the area, but very quickly had to admit there was nothing and nobody here.

Clean getaway.

"Hondo to Ten-David."

"Seventy-David, where the hell are you!"

Hondo blinked at the bark from Captain Fuller. "Sixth and Trenton. We lost contact below ground, Captain. Where's my backup?"

"Everything I have is going to Hawthorne Airport. Someone flipped on the runway lights. That's where Gamble and T.J. are heading."

"We're ten minutes away," Hondo snapped. "Request a black-and-white for pickup!"

"Negative. You stay right where you are! That's an order."

Hondo didn't bother to respond. While Street and the others watched, he simply dropped his radio to his side.

"Looks like they're trying to fly him out of here."

"Why would they bother to turn on landing lights and warn everyone?" Sanchez asked.

Street agreed. "There's a full moon out. A rookie pilot could land on a night like this. Gamble's smarter than that."

"And if he's going to Hawthorne," Hondo added, "why'd he pop up here?"

Street simply filled in, "Why's Fuller sending every man we got to Hawthorne?"

"Well, I'm not sitting around here to find out."

"Orders are to stay put," Street mentioned.

"Sometimes," Hondo said, "doing the right thing ain't doing the right thing."

Making the decision they all hoped for, Hondo held up his shield at a pair of approaching headlights and hurried right out into the middle of the road.

"Police!" he shouted. "Out of the car!"

"Hey, what's going on?"

The driver of the limousine that pulled over poked his head out the window of the enormous stretched vehicle and looked like a morsel of food being carried by a really big dog.

Hondo stuck his shield in the guy's face and said,

"Police emergency! I need your vehicle. I'll get it right back to you."

"Sergeant," Jim Street called from one of the passenger doors, "you better have a look in here."

Hondo dipped his head and peered into the acre of car. Peering back at him were eight high school seniors decked out in the splendor of pastel gowns and rented tuxes, freckled faces, hair gel, and too much makeup.

"All right, everybody out!" Hondo barked. "Move!"

Piles of tulle and satin rolled out of the vehicle and the S.W.A.T. team rolled in, Hondo getting behind the wheel before anybody else could call it.

"Who knew we'd be going to the prom?" Deke grumbled as he pulled a can of beer out from between the seats.

The kids would be on their own. But what a story they'd have to tell their grandkids.

In minutes the limo was moving along the expressway, with the widest visibility range available in this part of town. Everybody was on lookout. Hondo's face was grim, his hands firm on the wheel. Street in the passenger seat, fighting off déjà vu from just a little while ago. The door at his right elbow, Boxer behind him . . . the memories were too close. He wished he were driving.

He cast Hondo a glance. "I thought you didn't drive."

"I don't *like* to drive," Hondo corrected. "Kept getting into too many accidents."

Street hunkered down and pulled his seat belt on.

They didn't really know what they were looking for, so they went around in a couple of loops, assuming that Gamble hadn't come out that particular manhole in order to make things harder on himself. He wanted to be on this side of town for a reason. They just had to figure out the reason.

"Isn't that thing flying kinda low?" Sanchez spoke up from the luxury seats in back.

Street peered out the side window.

"That thing's getting ready to land!" Deke agreed.

Finally Street saw what they were talking about—landing lights. A fancy-looking jet, probably private, flying low and very slowly.

Hondo spoke up then. "Hey, Sanchez, how wide is the Sixth Street bridge?"

"You think I run around the barrio with a tape measure?"

"Gotta be four lanes across," Deke supplied. "Plane's small enough . . . might be able to set down."

Street leaned forward and brought his radio to his lips. "This is Ten-David-Seventy, we have visual confirmation of a low-flying plane headed for the Sixth Street bridge!"

17

THE LIMO WAS MOVING BUT GOOD. IN FACT THEY BLEW through three red lights in succession, one by crossing into the oncoming lanes, then swerving back in time to miss the astonished traffic stopped on the other side.

Well done, but the limo almost flipped on the rebound.

Hondo whipped the enormous car around a couple of pokey white-hairs in a Regal, then swerved again around a pickup. Amazing that a half acre of car could hinge in the middle. Street glanced back. Deke's eyes were real big and Sanchez's fingers were turning white as she hung on.

"We can see DWP workers who've blocked off that bridge with orange cones," Street continued into his radio. "You can bet they're not real DPW. Do you copy?"

In his mind he could imagine the cops at Hawthorne Airport yanking up stakes and bulleting out of there, feeling like idiots for having been so easily misled. Not only that, but on top of feeling stupid they stood a good chance of missing all the action when it finally blew.

"The plane's landing! Can you see it?" Sanchez called from the back.

Street craned to look through the glittering night at the Sixth Street Bridge, lit up like a Christmas tree. Never in his life had he wanted to sprout wings and rise over the streets and obstacles, stores and parking lots that stood between them and the bridge.

The jet landed hard, taking up almost the whole bridge to screech to a stop. The pilot must be standing on those brakes for all he was worth.

"They'll have to turn around to take off." Street said, thinking aloud. "That gives us time."

"I ain't making any assumptions," Hondo said, cranking the wheel hard again and throwing them sideways.

"Pretty impressive landing," Deke said. "That money's at work already. He's got the best pilots, for sure."

"Probably the same assholes who taught the terrorists how to fly into the World Trade Center," Sanchez bitterly commented.

"Connecting some pretty flimsy dots there, Christine," Street told her.

"There's only one dot I want to connect," she said. "The one on top of T.J.'s goddamned head."

Street squared himself in his seat and felt the

weapon in his hands grow warm and ready just from his own burning disgust. "Amen to that."

"Give them the details," Hondo prodded. "Never mind. Hold the radio up for me. Ten-David, this is Seventy-David! He's not coming into Hawthorne! We're currently in pursuit."

"I gave you an order to stand down!"

Oops. Fuller.

"Well, I would have," Hondo snapped, "except I noticed a Lear jet about to land on the Sixth Street bridge, Tom."

"What—Keep your distance and observe till I get some men down there to verify—"

"That'll be too late."

Street lowered the radio. "Well, he's in the loop now, I guess, isn't he?"

Hondo wheeled the limo in a crazy curve around a bend. This car had the turning radius of Ohio, but he was forcing it to squeak through places where there really weren't places. For a guy who didn't like to drive he sure knew how to do it.

"Get the plane turned around!"

Men on the bridge in DPW attire rushed to fulfill the pilot's order as Brian Gamble, T. J. McCabe, Travis, and Alexander Lupin drove up in the Suburban. Nick would tie up loose ends here and meet them in the Caribbean.

Not that anybody really cared. Money like Lupin's made a lot more enemies than friends, and made friends expendable.

Several cars had backed up as they approached the bridge from the west and were immediately passed through the cones by the fake DPW guys.

"Guy's worth every penny," Gamble commented, glancing at Lupin.

Lupin grinned, satisfied and smelling his freedom. "I'm ready to go home."

Within moments the next step of the plan went into play. T.J. and Gamble rigged a cable to one of the aircraft's rear landing gear and attached it to the Suburban, while Travis put Lupin inside the plane.

Gamble took the Suburban's wheel and began slowly backing up, turning the plane on the cleared four lanes and taking care not to scuff the wings on the bridge supports.

"Ninety seconds and counting," he ticked off into his handheld radio.

Travis gave him a hand signal then, and Gamble stopped. He waited, not exactly patiently, as the cable was detached and hooked to the other landing gear, with which they could then complete the turnaround. Then Travis detached the cables, Gamble moved the Suburban out of the way, and together they ran to board the plane. Gamble threw a cocky wave at the confused and amazed people now standing outside their cars, behind a blockade of orange cones. They were making up all kinds of scenarios in their minds. Wonder which one came up with the correct idea?

Now the plane had a completely clear runway— the entire expanse of the bridge.

There was nothing in their way.

Inside the plane was a terrified good-looking lady maybe in her fifties, and her husband, probably, a businessman of some kind, judging from the suit and the fact that this was probably their plane. They didn't look like rock stars, so they'd very likely just earned their way here the hard way. It happened.

Gamble reflected on his own way of getting here. He'd earned that to. Just quicker.

"Only room for one of you," he said, counting the seats. He looked at the man and said, "Be a gentleman get out."

"I'm not getting off this plane without my wife," the man said defiantly.

Alex Lupin moved in like a mongoose, grasped the man's head, and snapped his neck.

The woman screamed, "Richard!" but it was too late. Just like that.

Lupin tossed the man's body out of the plane's boarding hatch. "Richard's gone. Sit down and shut up."

Gamble watched impassively, but this actually did strike him as unnecessary. Oh, well.

He reached over and closed the hatch. "Let's go," he called to the pilots.

The jet began to taxi, although it wouldn't exactly have room to mosey into position.

"Van One, Van Two," he spoke into his radio, "we're clear. Good job, people. See you in Margaritaville."

259

"Roger that."

"Have a nice trip."

He closed off, then handed a cell phone and a sheet of paper to Alex Lupin as the plane began to rev around them.

"What's this?" Lupin asked.

"The account number where I want the money. When my bank verifies the transfer, you're a free man."

Lupin's smug smile fell away.

He was really just in a whole other kind of custody. Now he was realizing that.

"When this is all over," Lupin attempted, "I'd like you to come and work for me."

Gamble shook his head with distaste at the idea. "After you make that transfer," he said, "I won't need a job."

He sat down in a seat through which he could just barely see one end of the bridge. He took out a second cell phone with a satellite connection and punched in some key numbers.

On the end of the bridge Van 1 quite simply and perfectly blew itself into a fireball.

One batch of mouths silenced.

Then he began impassively to punch in the code that would blow up the second van. No loose ends.

So much for loyalty.

Half mile and closing. The limo roared.

"Can you catch the tail number?" Hondo bellowed.

Street peered through binoculars at the Learjet on the bridge.

"Suspects have entered the aircraft," he uttered. "Tail number is . . . N 51 . . . OJC."

"Confirm N51OJC," the dispatcher recited.

"Affirmative," Street confirmed.

"Stand by, Seventy-David."

"Shit, did you see that?!" Deke blurted.

But they'd all seen it. A huge explosion on one end of the bridge! Flame and wreckage mushroomed high into the air, engulfing several cars that had been stopped.

Only a few seconds later there was another explosion, this one on the other side of the bridge. Like a giant smoldering bracket, the bridge looked as if it would break loose on both ends and take flight with fire on its wings.

Street and Hondo and the others just stared as the limo closed on the immediate area of the mayhem.

"R-ten to Seventy-David," Velasquez's voice came through. "There are hostages on board. Proceed with extreme caution."

"All right," Hondo said, "you heard the man. Let's use caution."

What a joke.

He proved it by slamming down the accelerator and hurtling right toward the burning wreckage, and right into it. The limo made a god-awful grinding noise as it burst through the wall of fire and ruin and burst out onto the bridge with a thud.

"If they get off the ground, the hostages are

dead," Hondo said quickly. "This is the real thing, boys! And girl! They get off the ground, those hostages are dead!"

Grinding on past the wreckage, scratching against the cement breaker wall, the limo made a terrible noise.

Sanchez used the remote to open the sunroof, then without a beat she climbed up and poked her head—and her weapon—out. She was already aimed when the cool wind hit her, and she took five well-considered shots at the wings of the plane, then two more at the engines. The rounds hit the targets, but the plane kept going, and kept lifting.

"It's no good, Hondo!" she called down.

In his mind, Street could hear the reactions from inside the plane—shouts to get the assault team off their asses so they could take off and realize their plans for a life of unbelievable wealth in a foreign country. The idea turned his stomach and steeled his brain.

He had his own head out of the sunroof beside Sanchez's leg when he saw something she didn't— the door of the moving plane scratched open and Street was confronted with the unbelievable sight of Brian Gamble leaning out, taking aim—

Dink! A bullet whanged the windshield.

The limo swerved and Sanchez was thrown down on top of Street.

"No, problem," Hondo called. "The whole driving thing's coming back to me."

*   *   *

Inside the aircraft, a refrigerator was jostled by a jolt to the left. The door opened and a bottle of Cristal rolled out to bump against Alex Lupin's foot.

"How appropriate," he said, and picked up the bottle.

"Don't pop it," T. J. McCabe said, "till we're over the Pacific."

The jet's engines began to whine. Climbing . . . lifting, leaving the pavement beneath . . .

Suddenly the aircraft suffered a jolt that threw Lupin against the bulkhead.

"Get us up!" he shouted, clinging to his Cristal.

"Come on!" Brian Gamble shouted at the same time.

"Almost there!" the pilot strained, even his words working.

Lupin pulled himself back to balance and looked out the nearest window.

He did not see the Pacific, or even the lights of Los Angeles beneath him.

What he saw was the black side of a limousine, a row of wide windows, and the faces of those who would stand in his way.

For the first time, confidence failed him as he looked in their eyes.

The private jet accelerated away from the limo like a bird on the escape. The plane began to lift off, its wheels dropping slightly as it rose three feet . . . five . . . seven . . .

Hondo yanked the limousine alongside the jet,

then jogged to the side and made a good solid slam against the landing gear. The occupants would get a good jolt from that!

Street felt the wind on his face and the jet wash and squinted against the roar of the plane. He, Deke, and Sanchez were outside now, all of them, all clinging to the top of the limousine, weapons shouldered. Street was gladly the first to open fire on the plane's engines. *Pok pok pok!*

The jets whined and struggled, making a terrible scream against the night over the concrete culvert. They heard the howl increase as the pilots tried to go for it, to get the plane into the air even sooner. Jet exhaust began to scorch the uniforms of all three riding on top.

Again Brian Gamble appeared and took a shot at the windshield in front of Hondo. Luckily, the glass didn't crackle, but just took the dent.

Hondo slammed on the brakes and dropped behind the aircraft while Street and Sanchez hung on for dear life, and Street reached over in a flailing grab and caught Deke before he ended up in the river or somewhere even worse. Hot jet exhaust reddened their straining faces.

Hondo swung around the other side of the aircraft and began gaining again with the same second. From here, even Hondo could stick his handgun out and shoot.

So they did. All four of them opened up on the plane's nearest engine. The engine obliged by grinding and sputtering pitifully.

The plane went higher in spite of its damage. They were taking off!

And they could—not well—but they could fly with one engine.

No! Street cried in his mind, or maybe he actually said it out loud, but who could hear? He opened fire again, and this time he didn't stop.

Suddenly the plane began to falter. A wing tipped—caught a street lamp!

The limo screeched slowly again just as the plane whipped full around, slammed back down onto the bridge, and began sliding the rest of the way backward toward the end of the bridge.

Hondo hit the brakes. Street, Sanchez, and Deke watched in shock as the jet hit the edge of the bridge's north side and began horridly to roll over, crashing now into several power lines paralleling the bridge.

A hail of sparks blew high and wide. Caught like a bug in a web, the plane now hung over the deep cement culvert below. It was a long, long drop.

And a miracle save. The jet just hung there, looking like something inside a Fourth of July sparkler. A moment later, the engine was on fire, and the fire was blooming.

The jet's door popped open again. Brian Gamble appeared, dragging a civilian woman as a human shield.

Street jumped out of the limo and went after them on foot.

Meanwhile, Sanchez caught the second guy, that Travis guy, as he bailed out onto the bridge.

"Freeze!" she challenged.

He didn't. In fact he turned and pumped two rounds into her leg.

As she went down, Officer Sanchez of S.W.A.T., the first woman of her kind, returned fire in perfect form, even as she fell. With three perfect shots all in the vermilion line, she slaughtered the heartless criminal as her training and this moment's morality dictated.

He hit the pavement, already dead.

"Sanchez!" Deke called.

Street saw that a team member was down and turned back to go to her.

"We got her!" Hondo shouted to him. "Get Gamble!"

As Street broke to resume his pursuit, Hondo held on to Sanchez by one arm and watched as one of the bad guys fired on his men. It made him mad. Silly, maybe, but this had become way too personal.

Hondo saw what Street did not as he ran after Brian Gamble, probably with his own brain on fire with some kind of retribution. From here Hondo knew Street was about to be killed by the human scum behind him.

"Bad idea," Hondo mumbled. He raised his weapon and fired on instinct—no time to aim. Three shots—*pop, pop, pop.*

The man went down, rolled, and didn't move again.

Hondo turned to Sanchez. "You still breathing?"

"Kevlar took the hit," she gasped, the air driven from her by the impact. She winced—probably from the heat. "Don't stop for me!"

18

Moments later Hondo and Deke ran toward the flaming wreck of the fancy aircraft, primed to shoot. Alexander Lupin and T. J. McCabe came rushing out from the plane, then broke in two different directions.

Hondo was there when Alex Lupin ran out of bullets and decided to break right toward the body of his dead hired gun. He was going for the dead guy's weapon!

The S.W.A.T. cops ran faster, but Lupin couldn't get the gun out from under the guy's dead weight, so took the man's knife instead.

A knife? Who was he kidding?

Deke got there first, simply knocked the knife out of his way, and greeted Lupin with a fist in the face. In moments the felon was moaning and in cuffs. A knife. Sheesh.

"Damn, there goes the mansion in Beverly Hills," Deke commented. When the skinny crime boss tried to rise, there was a S.W.A.T. boot in his back.

"Did I tell you to get up? You're just another prisoner now, asshole."

Hondo skidded up beside them, but restrained himself from stomping the guy's face all the way into the pavement. He also ended up proud of himself for holding back. Nobody would crucify him if he didn't. But you're either on the side of the law or you're not.

As Deke hauled the creep into custody, Hondo looked up in time to see T.J. just standing there on the littered pavement of the bridge.

Deke blocked T.J.'s path to freedom. Deke's .45 was aimed right at T.J.'s heart.

"Why, T.J.?" Deke asked.

T.J. just stood there as if trying to decide which magazine to buy.

"I don't know," he said, his voice rough. "Thought we'd get away with it. Didn't know he'd hit Boxer. Figured piña coladas on the beach the rest of my life . . . never wanted it to turn . . . God-damn it, Sarge . . ."

Hondo approached with his gun out. As he came closer, T.J. saw him and simply raised a handgun to his own head.

"T.J.," Hondo began slowly, "this isn't how it ends."

"I can't come back from this."

"Now, listen to me, son—"

"Nothing left to say," T.J. offered, "except I'm sorry."

Hondo held out a hand. "No reason to make things even sorrier. Think about all the—"

There was a gunshot. It pounded through the night, all by itself. Blood and brains made a sad declaration about the success or failure of some plans, some dreams.

The shot might as well have hit them all. S.W.A.T. was about saving souls, no matter how lost.

On the far end of the Sixth Street Bridge, Jim Street found Brian Gamble waiting for him. Gamble had Mrs. Segerstrom neatly bundled with a rope around her waist, and was keeping cover behind the terrorized woman as he slipped the rope through a slot in the bridge to the concrete below.

Street approached almost peacefully, his weapon raised.

"Did you teach me how to play this game, Bri?" he asked. "Bullet through her shoulder, straight into your heart?"

"All you gotta do is pull the trigger." Gamble kept working on his rope.

Street took aim. The woman was perfectly petrified, but to her credit she took a breath and held it, waiting for the shot. She didn't coil up or try to pull away.

That's trust.

Street had the shot, but only through the hostage's body. He could've made it. He could.

Gamble saw him make the choice and took advantage. He jumped, and scaled down the rope, using the lady as a counterweight.

Now Street ran to the edge of the bridge. All bets were off again.

Gamble fast-roped down off the bridge into a rail yard in the darkness below. As he went, he aimed his M-4 up at Street, who ducked just in time. The rattle of Gamble's weapon was perfectly awful. He was really shooting, emptying his weapon at his former partner and best friend.

Seemed impossible that this moment had actually come. Guess the old Brian was really gone. Dead. Killed by this new one.

"Sorry, ma'am," Street said quickly, "but I need your help."

"Please—no," she pleaded. "Enough!"

"It's all right, ma'am. We're the good guys."

Making the bet that Gamble had actually emptied that weapon, Street swung over the side, using the woman as a counterweight just the way Gamble had.

And down he went.

Below was a maze of train engines and rail cars. Gamble dropped the distance to the ground and touched down amid the idling trains.

Street dared to fire at him as he rappelled, but missed. He kept an eye on Gamble, who disappeared into the darkness, and that was a mistake. Instead of watching where he was going, he watched Gamble. His arm struck a train car. The impact sent a jolt from his elbow to his shoulder, and sent the gun in his hand flying. He never saw where the gun landed, and he landed awkwardly, jarring his hip and knee.

Rolling, he came up limping and took off after Gamble, ignoring his own pain—hard to do because it was his knee and hip joint that hurt and he needed them. As he ducked and weaved between cars, his leg began to forget about itself and limber up.

A shadow!

He ran to it. Nothing. He stopped, listened.

A tiny crunch. Gamble!

Running!

Street broke out of hiding and ran furiously, pouring everything he had into eating the ground under him. Gamble was running too, and knew better than to look back.

Down the tracks they went like two collegiates in a competition, until Street's fingers lanced outward and he managed to hook two of them in Gamble's collar.

Then he pulled and they both went down, tangled up and thrashing. Their own speed carried them in a slapping roll down the tracks, which lashed at their clothes and brutalized their faces and hands. They came out bruised and bloodied, and laid into each other.

Brutal kicks and uncompromising blocks, punches, and slams erupted as if they were two tornadoes crashing into each other. A dozen trained moves and a dozen more improvisations made them a terrible match for each other. Some of these moves they had actually taught each other, in a hundred happy practice sessions between partners and friends. Now the bitter feud laid itself open like a wound.

The blows landed on Street's body like hammer hits, but he couldn't feel them. Something had taken over that protected him from his own pain—perhaps only a larger pain. He was relentless. Nothing could drive him down. He wasn't going down.

Strike after strike, he returned and redoubled Gamble's hits until Gamble began finally to weaken. Street would never know whether it was the physical part of Brian that began to fade or the mental burden of knowing what he had done, what he had become.

By the time Street finally overpowered him, neither cared what the answer was.

The blows stopped. Weak and bloody, Gamble backed off a step.

"Guess it's too late to call this thing a draw," he said, then spat blood onto the rails.

Street staggered, catching his breath. "Yeah."

They each sucked a gasp to steady themselves, and lunged at each other. The battle was on again. Gamble landed a good head-butt on Street, but Street knew it was coming. He used Gamble's head like a speed bag, and that was all he needed.

Gamble sank to the rails, out cold. Yes, Gamble had taught him that countermove. Sad, sad.

He shoved Gamble over with his foot, and cuffed him.

Stumbling with weakness and knotted with aches and bruises, he used the last of his strength to haul Gamble up onto his shoulder and took a beat to regain his equilibrium. His head turned like a Lazy Susan. He tried to counterturn, and staggered. The weight of Gamble over his shoulder seemed to be pulling him along.

Come on, old buddy. Salvation is around the corner and up the hill. Mine, not yours.

19

SIXTH STREET BRIDGE
Twenty minutes later

THE SCENE HAD TRANSFORMED COMPLETELY. THE BURNING plane was now a smoldering soaked mess surrounded by fire department personnel and pumpers. Feds were everywhere, as were ambulances and patrol units, and the coroner's wagon. Not pretty.

But a win for S.W.A.T.

Street had just delivered Gamble into FBI custody and now limped toward his team members, his partners on the team that had saved this awful day.

Hondo surveyed his battered form. "Street . . . man, get in an ambulance or something."

"Shift's not over yet, Sarge," Street rasped.

Emotionally, physically—was there anything else? Psychologically? He was whipped, drained.

Luckily, he was rescued from the awkward moment when Captain Fuller and Lieutenant Velasquez approached them.

Hondo didn't wait for polite exchanges. "How's Boxer?"

Street perked up for the first time.

"Got word he's going to pull through," Velasquez said.

The knees suddenly got thready under Street's weight. He wished he had something to lean on.

"Thank God," Sanchez whispered.

Fuller glanced around at the terrible scene, knowing he had something to say but stalling. Eventually he had to cough it up and bothered to face the team, at least.

"Nice work."

"You expecting something less?" Hondo popped back.

"We've still got a problem," Fuller went on, running over his own more-or-less apology, and pointed at the well-shackled Alex Lupin. "He's still in L.A."

Hondo looked among the others. "Any ideas?"

TWENTY-NINE PALMS UNITED STATES MARINE BASE

Located in a sea of desert, the small military base could easily be defended from any direction, just as the designers had intended.

In the fetal glow of dawn, four Marine MPs approached a S.W.A.T. truck followed by four black-

and-white patrol cars. The back doors of the truck flew open and four S.W.A.T. cops jumped out, and dragged a rather nondescript man out with them.

They pushed this man to the MPs, who gladly took charge of the international criminal whose days of power were over.

"Thank you, sir," the Marine sergeant said. "You have a good day, now."

Hondo Harrelson was almost asleep as the S.W.A.T. truck headed back toward the expanse of Los Angeles. For now the road was lonely, the desert silent, and the day a pleasant one. They had stopped a blizzard of dirty money from flooding the crime market, and they felt good.

They were battered, exhausted. Around him, Deke, Sanchez, and Street were taking the drive as a chance to sleep. Hondo's own eyes were closed, and he was fading fast to the constant hum of the tires.

"All units, we have a 211 in progress at the Diamond Mart, 543 Hope Street. Shots fired."

Hondo cracked one eye open.

Jim Street was already sitting up straight. Sanchez nudged Deke awake.

What the hell.

Hondo sat up too, and gave their driver a nod.

"Duty calls," he said, "and it don't kid around."

The truck accelerated beneath them, rushing like a magic carpet toward the glittering city in the distance.

Another day, another S.W.A.T. against crime.

Visit
❖ Pocket Books ❖
online at

---

www.SimonSays.com

Keep up on the latest new
releases from your favorite
authors, as well as author
appearances, news, chats,
special offers and more.

SIMON & SCHUSTER
A VIACOM COMPANY
www.SimonSays.com

Pocket
Books

2381-01